G000150371

More praise for J

VINNIE GOT BLOWN AWAY

'This is a short sharp shock of a novel. Cameron renders the speech of
disaffected London youth better than anyone else.'
GQ

'Like some distant, downbeat relative of Anthony Burgess's A
Clockwork Orange, Jeremy Cameron's earthily gripping debut thriller
is a fast, funny trawl through the territory of London's new outlaw
underclass . . . a masterly piece of storytelling.'
Financial Times

'With a feeling for street life that renders it sexy and poignant,
uncommonly astute about crime and its causes.'
Literary Review

'Audacious and outrageous.'
Daily Telegraph

'Swaggering, steaming work.'
Nicholas Blincoe, The Guardian

'Very entertaining.'
Razor Smith, Prison Writing

'Extraordinarily effective in its depiction of a seedy criminal
underworld. This is Walthamstow's answer to the fifties pulp fiction
of the USA.'
What's On In London

IT WAS AN ACCIDENT

'A wonderful thriller . . . an absolute cracker, the superb narrative
voice, North East London streetspeak, is so convincingly done that it
makes the residents of Albert Square sound like Dick Van Dyke in
Mary Poppins.'
The Independent

'The pleasure is intense. Jeremy Cameron has an unmatched ear for the shady melodies of London's streets. A funny, violent tale.'
Time Out

'His street talk sizzles with wit and invention. Engaging, eventful and original.'
Literary Review

'A brilliant line in street patter that confirms Cameron as the Damon Runyan of North East London.'
New Statesman

'Cameron's hilarious novel is turbo-charged entertainment . . . Britain's sharpest, funniest crime writer.'
Big Issue

'Cameron has been compared to Roddy Doyle and it is easy to see why.'
The Observer

BROWN BREAD IN WENGEN

'Warm, engaging and shot through with genuine humanity.'
Probation Journal

HELL ON HOE STREET

'Consistently entertaining and funny . . . a real east meets west rollercoaster.'
The Times

Also by Jeremy Cameron

VINNIE GOT BLOWN AWAY
IT WAS AN ACCIDENT
BROWN BREAD IN WENGEN
HELL ON HOE STREET

Wider Than Walthamstow

Jeremy Cameron

Stow Books

First published in Great Britain by Stow Books, 2004

Copyright © Jeremy Cameron, 2004

This book is copyright under the Berne Convention.
No reproduction without permission.

The right of Jeremy Cameron to be identified as author of this work
has been asserted in accordance with sections 77 and 78 of the
Copyright, Designs and Patents Act, 1988.

Stow Books
1 Ivy Cottage
The Forest
London E11 1PJ

British Library Cataloguing in Publication Data
A CIP catalogue record for this book is available
from the British Library

This book is a work of fiction. Names, characters, places and
incidents are either a product of the author's imagination or are
used fictitiously. Any resemblance to actual people living or dead,
events or locales is entirely coincidental.

ISBN 0-9548130-0-6

Typeset by SX Composing DTP, Rayleigh, Essex
Printed and bound in Great Britain by
Cox & Wyman Ltd, Reading, Berkshire

Acknowledgements

With thanks to Sally Partington, Alice Mara,
Kerry Livingstone and Belinda Mara

ONE

I WAS ONLY STANDING in the queue for signing on when the geezer in front of me got shafted.

'Jesus,' I went. 'As if it don't take long enough already.'

Geezer in front of the geezer turned round and stuck him straight. Down he goes. First geezer walks off, probably comes back later for signing on or he misses his giro.

I got up the counter eventual after Old Bill did their various.

'Good cabaret,' I went to the bird behind the desk. Lighten the tone like.

'Shut the fuck up,' she turned round and said. Part of their special assistance measures up the Job Shop.

'Just my fucking luck,' I goes. 'Geezer got to get shafted before I signed on. Been stood here two bleedin' hours now. All them jobs I was just waiting to grab, they all gone up the swannee now, am I right?'

'Sign in the usual,' she goes.

'You reckon I got heavy trauma?'

'You'll get heavy trauma off me Mr bleedin' Burkett if you don't sign on sharp and fuck off out of here.'

I gave her a good butcher's.

'Louise?' I went.

'One and the same.'

Louise Bedworth I went to McEntee with. Passed her GCSEs there and now she got a number up the Job Shop.

'Louise, you reckon I can get the Sickness after I clocked a stabbing? Nervous debility? Get a book and don't have to come and sign on every fortnight?'

She made a noise. Very rude noise.

'Or Incapacity Benefit? Twenty quid a week on top? You witness my suffering lasting distress? Geezer standing right next to me gets totalled? Brown bread? Body bag situation?'

'Must be very stressful Nicky Burkett, some geezer getting stucked and you not being the geezer did it. Very stressful indeed.'

'Now Louise, be fair girl,' I went. She was digging me out here. 'I ain't never only stabbed a couple of geezers and not for years now innit? Be fair girl.'

'Sign fucking here Nicky.'

So I did.

Course then I only got to wait another two hours for Old Bill to finish up. Geezer who did the shafting he was long gone. Me, I wished I left straight after him, only you miss your signing on and they cut your dole right off, slightest excuse and there you were, potless.

It was some white geezer about twenty-five did the sticking and it was some other white geezer a bit older got stuck. They were strangers both. More than likely they just moved to the area. I'd been signing in that queue since I was in nappies and I never knew them.

Important point was it seemed like it was a hit. Professional.

How it happened was this. I was chattering Jimmy Foley who just came out of the Ville after a five month. Least he came out three weeks ago when he made his fresh claim, then he had to starve three weeks till he signed on again and they doshed him a giro. He reckoned he'd be glad of a giro so he could stop thieving food for a couple of days, it was tiring. So there we were gassing, this and that and who was in the Ville these days and the quality of the weed, not paying much attention, when out of my left mincer I clocked this geezer turn round and stab this other geezer.

He left the sticker in there and walked out. Wearing gloves so no prints.

Stabbed geezer turned round to me and Jimmy. First off he never knew what happened. You could tell he reckoned he got punched, never understood why it stopped him so hard. Then he put his mitts down and he felt the sticker and he clocked his mitts all covered in gravy and he knew he got very serious aggravation. Outside Charlie Chan's where you got most of your stabbings you got some messy one in the guts and you might stagger off and croak in the street or maybe you got lucky and it missed things and you finished up in Casualty. But this one was an up and under. Hard up into the heart. This was a hit. And the geezer knew he was gone.

'Jesus Nicky,' went Jimmy.

'Jesus Jimmy,' I goes.

Geezer's gob opened and his eyes went terrified.

He pulled out a little package. Gave it to me.

'Elena,' he gasped.

Then he went down dead.

'Jimmy don't touch,' I turned round and said.

We all cleared a space. Nobody wanted to know. He was out of it, no call for the kiss of life when he already got the kiss of death.

Few people cleared straight off. Rest stayed for their signing on. We all stood there standing.

Old Bill got there in three minutes after the alarm from the counter. Fucking hundreds of them.

Fortunate everyone knew what went down and ready to

be my witnesses. Otherwise they had me up the cells and gave me a kicking already.

'Nicky Burkett,' went DS O'Malley. One of the good guys up Chingford. In a manner of speaking. 'Fancy you being around when there's a stabbing you little fucker.'

'I want my brief,' I goes. 'You ain't getting nothing, I ain't got my brief.'

'You ain't done nothing Nicky from what I hear, what the fuck you want your brief for? Good citizen you only wanting to give evidence am I right apprehend the villain?'

'I want my brief.'

'Jesus Nicky you ain't half a tiresome little fucker. You're a witness mate. There ain't nothing in law says you're entitled to a solicitor present when you're a witness, you get me?'

'I want my brief.'

Tell the truth they never did stitch me up on a stabbing. Only ones they ever nicked me for, I did them, no complaints.

On the other hand there was always a first time.

'Get my brief here and I squeal like a pigeon,' I went.

'Fuck it. So who's your brief these days?'

'Mrs Mellow.'

'Mrs Mellow?'

'Mrs Mellow.'

He gave a no comment kind of comment. Mrs Mellow

was the caring type of lawyer. Never turned anyone down. Always see the good side in her clients. Even when they never had one.

I belled her office on the mobile.

'Nicky Burkett,' I goes to Aretha her receptionist.

'All right Nicky? What you done then?'

'Aretha I ain't done nothing. Mrs Mellow there or what I'm needing a verbal.'

'She ain't here Nicky, she on holiday.'

'Jesus. Where she gone?'

'Madeira I believe.'

'She pop back down the Job Centre for me?'

'I don't believe she can Nicky.'

'Shit. Who else you got?'

'What you wanting Nicky? We got all sorts. You want an international lawyer? Commercial? You want mortgage advice?'

'Do me a favour Aretha.'

'Family law? Or you setting up a company?'

'Aretha. . .'

'Can't be a criminal situation after all then Nicky surely?'

I got to cackle. She liked to wind up the punters. 'Aretha I come round there and give you a good smack you know that?'

'What you wanting then Nicky?'

'I just been witness to a murder up the Job Centre.'

'Jesus!'

'Old Bill want to interview me.'

'Jesus Nicky! That's terrible!'

'Yeah. I suffering extreme distress. Want Mrs Mellow to counsel my legal rights and stop me opening my gob wrong.'

'Nicky you want me to send her boy? Young Nigel?'

'Her boy?'

'Nigel Mathers. He just qualified. He quite a good boy. Need the experience too.'

I thought about it. 'Nah Aretha,' I went. 'I manage on my tod.'

I turned back to DS O'Malley. 'I manage without,' I went. 'Reckon I have Jimmy with me. That sweet with you?'

'Suit yourself Nicky. Have who you fucking like.'

So we went ahead and did the business. One thing they never had to look far for their witnesses. They got twenty of them standing all round, only me and Jimmy were the clearest. Just a question of doing the verbals.

Being the case it was straightforward, I never saw the need for telling how I got the package from the dead geezer in my jacket.

No point making their job easier. No idea the package helped them or not, only the way I clocked it we were paying our taxes to keep Old Bill in their suits so they might as well earn their pennies. I kept stum.

TWO

JIMMY FOLEY WAS A pavement trotter these days. But he never sold drugs like in the old days before CCTV. He never even retailed tobacco imports and lager like they did on Holloway Rd for all the gear they brought back from Calais. He was the middleman on travelcards.

He got some young bird nicking handbags. They borrowed the credit card, never touched anything else. They threw away the bag then they threw away the credit card after they used it. First it got remodelled by someone a lot cleverer than Jimmy. Same card new number. Then Jimmy got it back. Used it once and once only. Bought an annual travelcard about eight hundred quid. Retailed it for five, only changed the photo. Doshed a oner to the remodeller and another to the tealeaf bird. Left Jimmy with three. No losers, no harm done, down to the bank for paying the victim. Then for another half he sold the card on to some loser in a pub who tried to use it and got lifted.

By the second time it was too late. So no-one came looking for Jimmy on account of they already nicked someone for it and there was no point getting greedy.

Only problem was the fucking CCTV again. Best place for selling a travelcard was in a station, needless. Stick to the pavement or the precinct and he got lucky. Only Jimmy got careless. And then again he was a bit short in the brain area. So he went down the Central and he got fingered. CCTV destroyed the full time employment of many a pavement artist. Five months up the Ville.

'Officer I seen it!' Jimmy goes all excited now to DS O'Malley. 'I seen every bleeding fucking shitting stabbing thrust! This geezer he turns round and he cries out 'Die, drongo die! This is for me, this is for him, this is for her! This is for the honour of the fambly—'

'Jimmy,' DS O'Malley interrupted.

'Yes officer?'

'You ain't even the fuckin' witness here. You're like the witness to the witness. You're here to witness what we do with Nicky, how we treat him fair and don't brutalise him like he deserves. You're here to give him personal support in his time of distress, excuse me while I puke. Now shall we start the interview again?'

He tore up his notes, then he started in his notebook again with his sidekick listening, all of it in one of their recesses up the Job Shop where they gave you a hard time for not getting the job for a brain surgeon the only one they got advertised on their computer.

'Your chance come later Jimmy,' he goes.

'Oh all right officer. Long as you ringfence that contract.' Jimmy did a business start-up course in the Ville, knew the lingo.

So I gave it to them straight. Every moment, even the 'Elena'. Except the package that I never even took a butcher's at yet.

My problems were going to start when I got home to Noreen.

You got to understand how it was with Noreen.

First off I got my gaff. Least my mates got it for me when I came out from doing my time. Upstairs flat on Howard Rd, all nifty except when downstairs left the main door unlocked and undesirables got in, bailiffs and double glazing and Christians. I never got a gaff of my own before and I lay about drinking tea and watching videos. Then Noreen moved in.

Noreen was only the classiest, sexiest, most beautiful bit of thing in the whole borough. She was fucking lovely. She got a body like a banana. She got legs you just wanted to wrap round your shoulders and pray to. She got bosoms like a pistachio ice cream. Only that was never the whole of it. She got a great personality in the bargain. Like she was sweet and funny and affectionate and clever and forgiving.

Except when she turned nasty.

Then she was bitter and vicious and sarky and humpy like you never clocked in your whole life. She was like the CID and your worst teacher and the snooper from the Social all rolled into one. When she cut her mince pies at you and sucked her molars then boy there weren't no place to hide.

And there was more.

Before Noreen first got in my sheets, she got three certain things she made known.

First I got to take an AIDS test.

Then I got to wait two months for making sure I was clear.

Then I got to give up crime.

Most geezers, you give up crime means you never rob banks or bring in a shipload of brown. Noreen though she reckoned it meant not having no moody tax disc! Or bent MOT or retailing tobacco or sharing travelcards or working on the dole or drink driving or selling copy Nikes on the market! Noreen was pure, Noreen was straight, Noreen was a pain in the fucking arse sometimes. Except when she got up close and personal she was miss fucking goody fucking two shoes sex fiend and she made it all worth your while.

So I turned round and said all right. Took the test, waited two months till I was bursting and gave up all normal life like most geezers knew it.

Next she moved in.

Can't hardly say I ever asked her, I just found every morning when I woke up she was there. My mum reckoned I did something in some previous life, on account of nothing I did in this life deserved getting Noreen Hurlock for my bird. Kelly my babymother who I got little Danny with, that Kelly who left me for a German, she reckoned maybe Noreen was blind and deaf and got no sense of smell and mistook me for Robbie Williams. I told her if Robbie Williams got what I got he'd be a star. Sharon my sis, she was all right Sharon, she reckoned Noreen got convict fever, wanting some very bad geezer to cure. Jimmy Foley reckoned I got to have a bleeding great donger.

After Noreen moved in it got right civilised. We had her mum and dad round. She got both, a mum and a dad. Her brother was one of my mates from school. He was straight as well.

Noreen went to work. Every day. She got a number for British Airways up Regent St. She did computers at school then went to college then got a job with the Council then a travel agent down the market then they snapped her up for BA. Put her near the window for a bit playing her computer and they near as got flooded out with punters buying flights all over the Caribbean. She was still there in that office, working up the back now and making serious paper.

By which time the problem starts to be obvious.

Before Noreen set up residence in my gaff I got Housing Benefit. I got Job Seeker's Allowance. Twice a week it seemed like they tried to squeeze me out down the Job Centre, knock me off the dole on account of they reckoned there were plenty jobs in Walthamstow. Like the sky was green with pink spots. Only so far I was too fucking clever for them. I went on a job search up Hampstead. I went for an interview for a stockbroker. I belled every job in the paper using their dog and bone. So they gave in and I picked up the bits they gave out once a fortnight. I managed. Long as I went round Mum's for my tea when the dosh gave out after eleven days. I got by.

All that went awol when Noreen moved her knickers in.

She was working. She was making notes. She could pay the rent and keep herself and keep me in the bargain. How they reckoned it. They also reckoned how anything else was illegal. One other thing you could be sure of, Noreen agreed with them.

So I had to stop signing on and she gave me a few pennies for my back pocket. Wedge for the edge. Never even keep me in weed.

What was a geezer to do to keep his respect?

Only one thing for it.

Sign on from his mum's.

They sent the giro to Mum's address, I had a little over

for housekeeping and a few necessities. Noreen always wondered how I managed so well on her dosh. Told her I was a good manager.

Problem being, course, Noreen never knew I was signing on from Mum's. Now I was waiting for Krakatoa when she found out.

Bound to be in the paper even she never heard before. Me being witness to a murder, little Bridget Tansley off the *Guardian* be there before you could say alibi. I thought of telling Noreen I was accompanying Jimmy, give him emotional support through the fortnightly trauma of signing on. She blow that one out for breakfast. And me too.

Oh dear, oh fucking dear. I headed for home, up Hoe St then turned into Church Hill. Jimmy yacking beside me chattering like there was no tomorrow. Nor yesterday or the fucking thereafter.

Then he got shot.

Just where we turned the corner on Church Hill there was this Asian bird walking up Hoe St. Tall, fit, strong. Long black hair. Pins like chair legs. Skin like Cadbury's. With Asian birds you never could say they got big knockers. Showed no respect. She was well proportioned. Like Canary Wharf.

'Jesus Jimmy you clock that?' I went slobbering. I stopped dead.

Jimmy went yattering on no stopping. He just discovered he went the wrong day up the Job Centre anyhow, no dosh till tomorrow so he was warped. Straight on to the bird and the curry he had last night. When Jimmy got started he never got easily distracted and he was already on three topics the dole and the bird last night and the curry after, so he never registered a fourth and he carried straight on walking.

And got shot in the side.

Just where it was me, except I stopped.

Fuck.

Geezer on Hoe St got a handgun. I clocked him holding it two hands in front of him like on the TV.

Jimmy went down. No more than a gasp. I went down in the bargain, flung myself behind him. Then I grabbed him and held him up against me. Between me and the shooter, human shield.

Geezer fired again. Missed.

Shit fuck fuck.

Jimmy was moaning. He was alive.

I was moaning out of fear. I burrowed right under Jimmy.

They fired again and Jimmy took one in the shoulder. I felt the blow. He went whoosh. Took another one in the thigh.

Fucking fucking fuck.

Then it stopped. We were lying on the pavement, me

half under Jimmy and him bleeding. And he was getting unconscious.

My heart was bumping so I could hear it. Shit fuck and fucking fuck. I started sobbing.

I hoped Jimmy was never totalled.

On the other hand, him living I kind of hoped he never found out how I used him in a crisis. True that was what your mates were for, help you out in a tight spot. Put it another way though, they were supposed to decide that themselves.

One more moment it was quiet. Then screams and running and sirens. Old Bill was there. Still busy up the Job Centre only Westbury Rd a hundred metres off so they came lickety.

I was shaking and shitless. I couldn't get out from under.

Then I pushed Jimmy off and lay there on my back. I was still whimpering.

It was DS O'Malley again.

'Jesus Nicky it follows you around don't it?' he went sympathetic.

'Fucking fucking fucking fuck . . .'

'You alive?'

'Fucking fucking fuck . . .'

'Where you hit Nicky?'

'I ain't hit.'

'You got blood all over.'

'Jimmy.'

'You sure?'

'Yeah.'

'Lie still. We get the ambulance. Jimmy's been hit then?' Observational skills they taught up Hendon Police College.

'Shit. Hey, Karen!' He got to call a woman Old Bill for the touching bit. 'Your first aid up to scratch or what?'

'Bugger that Sarge. I ain't done first aid since the Brownies. And blood makes me go funny.'

'Shit. Nicky you know what to do for shootings?'

'Apply a tourniquet mate. Stem the bleeding.'

'Right.' He made himself busy. Except he never got a fucking clue. Fortunate the ambulance was there straight after. It just left with the body from the Job Centre so it turned round and came back still carrying it.

I lay there.

They went to Jimmy. Did their bits and bobs.

'He alive?' I went

'Yeah. Losing blood. Trauma.'

'Safe on that one. Trauma never affect Jimmy. West Ham losing every week made him used to it. Stop the bleeding and he be right as rain.'

They put him in the cart and gave me the once over.

'Can't find nothing,' they turned round and said. 'Best you come with us though, check you out and you're bound to be suffering shock.'

'Shock ain't hardly in the starting gates mate. Likely

suffering very very severe nervous debility. I don't reckon I ever work again. I bell my brief, put in an early claim off the Criminal Injuries.' Then I remembered Mrs Mellow was away. 'And you being my witnesses on my trauma innit disability living allowance for life or what?'

Then would you believe it for real I passed away. Jimmy was never the brightest bulb on the Christmas tree, but my sensitivity left me vulnerable to dramatic change. So some psychiatrist reckoned anyhow when they did a report for me years ago up the juvenile court. I passed right out like a squaddy on parade. Next thing I knew I woke up in Casualty with some big strong nurse bird leaning right over me giving me a flash. Not all bad then. I got this thing about strong women. Specially strong women in uniform. I should have gone in the army.

THREE

THEY HAD ME curtained off. Up Whipps Cross they used curtains for walls, never afford the cement. I was lying on a trolley with my mince pies closed. It was all peaceful except for the terminals crying out a bit. Then what should I only bleeding hear but the dulcet tones of DS TT fucking Martin fucking Holdsworth out of Chingford CID.

'Jesus I passed over and went to hell,' I goes. 'DS fucking TT there to greet me. Still DS. Still not made DI after all the management courses and arse licking.'

They called him TT on account of his wheels. He got himself one great big fucking bike on account of a chopper was so cool. Only problem was it was cool about thirty years before he got one. It was freezing when he first mounted up.

'Do me a fucking favour TT,' I went. 'Fuck off.'

'Perhaps you would like a cup of tea and a samosa.'

Oh my Gawd. He was multi-cultural.

'Gimme DS O'Malley,' I went.

'Nicky I'm here to help,' he went. Yeah. Course. Latest policy up the Old Bill was helping. Community Policing got a lot to answer for.

'You may know that I am now liaison officer at Chingford for the Make The Streets Safe campaign. You and Jimmy are my first victims.'

'Jimmy still breathing?'

'I am very glad to say that Jimmy is still breathing. Both in and out. He is currently in the operating theatre having some adjustments made to his body but a hospital spokesperson advises that the prognosis is benevolent.'

I was too tired.

'TT,' I went again. 'Fuck off.'

Next time I woke up O'Malley was there again.

'Never reckoned I'd be happy to clock you again,' I turned round and said. 'Only after TT you're a fucking breath.'

'Gives it a bit of that, am I right?'

'Innit?'

A tropical storm hit Whipps Cross. Hurricane Noreen.

'NICKY WHERE YOU?'

Must have left work dinner time and taken a half day to come and give tender love to her man.

'I KNOW YOU ARE IN THERE!'

I hid under my blankets. Course I loved her that Noreen, only it seemed how sometimes love and fear came very close together.

'NICKY BURKETT WHERE YOU HIDING? DO I HAVE TO SEARCH THIS HOSPITAL?'

'Excuse me miss,' went some security geezer followed her in. He maybe reckoned he could quiet her noise.

'NICKY YOU MAKE YOURSELF KNOWN THIS MOMENT, YOU HEAR!'

I poked my mitt up out of the blankets and waved it feeble. Close to death. I asked them to leave Jimmy's gravy on me for when Noreen came visiting, only they insisted on mopping it. Still I looked a sicko.

She came and stood by my trolley.

First she took a proper butcher's like she never believed I was still breathing. Then she slung her arms round me and kissed all round my chops and started leaking, streaming all down her boat race. Then she pulled herself together and gave me some serious grief.

'Nicky what the fuck were you doing up that Job Centre?'

Half the borough was in Casualty up Whipps Cross. They got homeless came in on account of the heating. They

23

got all the Community Cares and the radio rentals who legged it out of the locked wards. They got all the people never got a doctor or couldn't wait half the year for an appointment. They got cabbies came in for a cup of rosie on their break. They got some young lad off the paper chasing a bit of news, murders or *East Enders* stars jumping the queue. They even got a few casualties. All of them earholing Noreen and me having a barney. Noreen having a barney.

'Seeking some job Noreen, right? Job Centre, right?'

'You seeking some job? Nicky, do I look like I'm retarded?'

'Look bleeding beautiful same as always Noreen.'

'I look like your kid Danny, believe everything you turn round and say?'

'Don't look nothing like Danny, Noreen. Too tall. Mind he's catching up.'

'I look like Jimmy Foley or fucking Rameez Ahmed, your criminal types?'

'Not at all neither like Jimmy nor Rameez, no way Noreen. Not one bit. And too bleeding beautiful like I may have mentioned.'

Cut no ice with Noreen.

'You been up that fucking Job Centre signing on illegal, am I right?'

'Not exactly Noreen . . .'

'False claim DSS fucking Job Seeker's don't-make-me-split-myself-laughing Allowance, yeah?'

'Well Noreen . . .'

'"Well Noreen" . . .?'

'Well Noreen, maybe sort of how some ways . . . being as how you sees it . . . not strictly job seeking every minute maybe. Anyhow no jobs in Walthamstow you knows that.'

'Not seeking no fucking job too right. Claim the fucking allowance though even though you ain't entitled while you living with me, am I right?'

'Noreen . . .'

'Probably signing on from your mum's address, am I right or am I right?'

'Noreen . . .'

'Yeah?'

Took a deep breath.

'Noreen, got to be true how I'm unemployed, right?'

'Yeah?'

'Except cooking and cleaning and doing all them bits I love to do for you 'cos you're so beautiful, yeah?'

Cut no fucking ice.

'Only, take my point, normal run of things unemployed means you get the jam roll, yeah? Entitled your benefit cheque?'

She sucked her molars and gave me the looks-could-kill.

Then I played my ace of tarts.

'Only after today Noreen no need for all that! I put in

for the Nervous Debility after my traumas! See the quack tomorrow. No need for all them minor problems about that address!'

Her little beadies closed on me and her pupils went like she was on the Persian rugs. She never seemed too impressed with my nervous debility. She froze up. Her little mouth took on rigor mortis.

Then the fear hit me proper. I clocked that look before. I went there. It was a terrible journey. No!

'Noreen,' I cried, 'you ain't going to withhold them conjugal rights?'

One moment I reckoned she might burst.

'Conjugal rights?' she went. 'Bleedin' conjugal rights you little tosser?'

'Er, yeah, Noreen, touch of the whatsits, you know?'

'Conjugal rights? Well, let me get this clear mister, ain't them conjugal rights something what comes by after you get conjugal? And ain't there as much chance you getting conjugal as me turning into a frog? Am I right?'

About the conjugal that was a relief. So she was never thinking about churching. About the frog I reckoned she got the storyline wrong only now was maybe not the time for mentioning it.

She turned on her little heels and she was out of that Casualty. Whoosh.

It looked like I was closing down my benefit claim.

FOUR

ALL THE SAME, when they discharged me I got a three month sick note off the doc. Lie low a few days but then you never know how it might come in handy.

Doc was some bird in a white coat never slept for three days so she sign anything, I should have got a lifetime's freebie. She asked what I wanted, Nervous Exhaustion or Severe Trauma. I asked Nervous Debility. Nervous Exhaustion, all you wanted was a good sleep. Trauma you got counselling, fuck that. Nervous Debility got no cure. Only one better was Chronic Fatigue Syndrome.

She gave me three months Nervous Debility.

Jimmy was in Intensive Care how you would be after

you got shot three times. I was never allowed in to see him. Gave me a break. Before I visited Jimmy I wanted to send an advance party, find out if he knew how I used him for a flak jacket. Maybe Jimmy never minded, reckon that's what mates were for. All the same I reckoned assess the situation first.

No point entering Noreen's programme just yet so I went round Mum's.

As usual Mum's was humming like a hairdresser's.

There was Mum and Kelly my babymother visiting and Sharon my sis. Both their kids at school and Mum's feller Shithead at work so they could do what women do. I heard them when I turned in the street.

I came in cautious.

'All right Nicky?'

'All right Nicky?'

'All right Nicky?'

Then they carried on yacking as before about shoes and sex.

One thing you got to know. Women liked sex. Even more than they liked doing it they liked yacking about it. Shoes shoes shoes. Sex sex sex.

Me, I reckoned I was a blue-blooded geezer and I liked to put it away as much as the next man. I reckoned I knew how to oil their wheels in the bargain. I never got any complaints. On the other hand I knew there was other things in life besides sex. A good pint and a curry for starters.

Birds though, they were different. They wanted it all the time. Turn away from them one time in the night even when you were asleep and you got such a jab in the kidneys you reckoned it was a stabbing.

Noreen gave me one night off per week. Fridays she went up her mum and dad's. Me, I went playing pool with her brother Ricky and Elvis Littlejohn and Dean Longmore and Mercedes Marty Fisherman and Jimmy Foley. She sometimes stayed her mum's when it was late. Me, I got pissed and finished up under the pool table in the boozer. Anyhow Noreen gave me the night off.

The rest of the week I got to do the business. On demand. Pull my handle and three bells came up.

So I was always kind of fatigued. When I came round Mum's I was hoping for a spot of P and Q. Only what did I ever get? Talk about sex. Mostly not in front of me, what with it being Mum and my sis and my ex-bird, kind of tricky. Before and after and when I went in the toilet they were at it like a road drill.

'You know what that Karen turned round and said?'
'What?'
'What?'
'She reckoned she had better off a stick of celery and a Barry White CD!'
'She never!'
'She did!'

'And his idea of foreplay was "you want salt and vinegar or nice and spicy girl?"'

'He never!'

'He did!'

'She reckoned he never fell asleep after, he fell asleep just thinking about it!'

'He never!'

'He did!'

How I clocked it, birds and geezers, they were never compatible.

I went in my old room for a little lie down. Tell the truth I was feeling kind of queasy. Never liked to admit it after witnessing a stabbing and a shooting but I wasn't as young as I used to be and these things kind of got to you. Teenage you took them in your stride. After twenty-one you got feelings of mortality.

But no sooner I lay down for a snooze when the mobile went.

'Nicky,' he went loud. He never could do quiet.

'Jesus TT,' I went. 'Leave it out, right? Feller get a bit of peace after trauma or what?'

'Nicky we need to talk. Urgent.'

'You need to talk TT. I don't fucking need to talk to no-one.'

'Nicky we found out who the victim is.'

'Yeah?'

'And there's a reward.'

'A what?'

'Up front. Notes.'

'Grassing up some geezer?'

'Nicky you get down the boozer tonight, meet me and O'Malley and the DI?'

'Jesus TT the fuck you want me for?'

'Tell you down there.'

'I bring a witness.'

'Bring Noreen Nicky. Sensible woman, not like your mates, give you good advice.'

'I think about it.'

'Be in the Village about ten.'

'The Village. Never a copper's boozer, am I right?'

'Why we go there Nicky. Reckon we're college teachers or you're some IT merchant, all look about twenty and need new shoes.'

'Check you TT.' I cut him.

Next on the dog was Noreen. No sooner I lay down again.

'Nicky who was you talking to when I want you? You always on that mobile, give you radiation you know that?' She seemed to be forgetting last time we spoke we were never speaking again.

Told her what happen.

'Jesus Nicky what he want?'

'Fuck knows Noreen. You be there?'

'Right. You bringing anyone else?'

31

'Bridget Tansley.'

'Yeah . . .' Bridget Tansley was like out of my class, still she was a bird so Noreen got some doubtings.

'And Rameez.'

She cackled. 'Cover all options right?'

'Right.' Bridget Tansley off the *Walthamstow Guardian*. Rameez was the local baron. Between them they got all the news. Or they could make it.

I belled little Bridget. Got her home number. She reckoned it was worth giving it on account I was going to get her a job on the nationals one day. Specialist in stabbing.

She answered on the fifth bell.

'All right Bridget?' I goes.

'Nicky Burkett!'

'One and the same Bridget. What you doing?'

'Yoga Nicky. Excuse me, I just have to get upright.'

'You putting your little body in them positions?'

'Never mind what positions I'm in Nicky, your mind is disturbed enough already.'

'Who me?'

'Such a pleasure to talk to you, Nicky.' She was a little beauty was Bridget. Not a bad looker and she got all her bits in the right places. Did her journalism course and got lucky on her first earner, might have started anywhere but went right to the top with the *Walthamstow Guardian*.

'Bridget, I need your services like.'

'Confidential Nicky? Or News?'

No such thing as confidential with Bridget. Question was, this week or next.

'Dunno yet Bridget. Pick you up at yours?'

'You little charmer Nicky, I bet you would.' One thing about Bridget, she never did tell me where her gaff was. Some place up South Woodford I reckoned from her number. Like half the people who worked in Walthamstow she came in for the job then fucked off out again soon as she finished. Into Essex most of them, fast as their jeeps could take them. Still Bridget never went far, kept on our side of the North Circular. I hated the fucking geezers the other side.

'You could knock me up a spot of nosh Bridget, touch of the curry and salad to go with that yoga, yeah?'

'I think you might be getting confused with yoghurt Nicky. There isn't any set meal with yoga as far as I know.'

'Same difference Bridget, you knock me up a bit of this and a bit of that and then we get down the boozer.'

'It will be a pleasure to meet you there Nicky. Where and when?'

'Village Bridget. Up Orford Rd.'

'I know where the Village is. What time?'

'Ten. You be there?'

'What's it about?'

'Got to meet TT and some other fucking DS, O'Malley, and some fucking DI.'

'This sounds big Nicky. Is it about this murder?'

'Got to be. Don't know the fuck more.'

'I'll be there.'

'Mine's a pint of lager Bridget, seeing as you being on expenses.'

'And you'll get another one off the police I expect since they're on expenses too.'

'You read me like a mirror Bridget.'

'I'll look forward to seeing you there Nicky.'

Such a little body that Bridget. Get as far with her as I could throw a boomerang.

FIVE

RAMEEZ WAS A different matter now.

Mornings and early evenings Rameez was unobtainable. Mornings he was sleeping. Rameez believed how any baron worth the price of an Audi needed eight hours sleep minimum. So he slept from three till eleven. Then he got four cups of tea with his sugar puffs. Then he relaxed until twelve when the afternoon came. Afternoons were business. He went round threatened a few shops, took the protection, then he retailed a couple of motors and a few electricals and a bit of charlie. Never very keen on the brown was Rameez, preferred charlie and Es. Then he drove round and about the manor letting himself be seen. Business meant you got to be seen. Geezers could be coming to him with problems. Rameez gave out justice. So he had to be public.

Early evenings were relaxation again. Before serious work started, dealings and stabbings and that, Rameez he needed to relax. Later might be some club up Clapton for business. Early evening though when he was unobtainable he got two choices. Either he was putting it up some blonde bit round her place. Or he was down the boozer kind of incognito. Just now these last few weeks he gave his custom to the Victoria up Hoe St.

Up the Victoria Rameez was as incognito as you could get. Never a special problem being Asian, the Victoria was never a prejudiced boozer. Least it was never prejudiced special against Asians. It was prejudiced in a manner of speaking against the whole world except a little bit of land between Wales and America. I never got any aggravation in there. Only problem was I never understood Gaelic football and I never understood hurley and sometimes I never understood a fucking word any geezer in there turned round and said.

When I went to the cinema next door on Hoe St I liked to pop in before for a Red Bull and a few shorts. Then you could get in after the show about ten to eleven for a few pints before closing. Rameez was likely to be on Pernod. I went up the stairs and found the way through the dark into the bar, never easy. I got a couple of drinks and there was

Rameez settled in his corner with Aftab and Afzal and Javed. They were relaxed nicely nicely, taking an intelligent interest in the football on the satellite and reminiscing about blonde birds.

'All right Rameez?'

'All right Nicky?'

'All right Aftab?'

'All right Nicky?'

'All right Afzal?'

'All right Nicky?'

'All right Javed?'

'All right Nicky?'

You got to do it in the right order or they got insulted. Very strong on honour were Rameez and his boys. Disrespect his mum or his heavies or his Audi and you got a very severe slicing.

'Good to clock you Rameez.'

'Good to clock you Nicky.'

'Good . . .' Nah, I reckoned I could skip the others on this one.

'Which team you fancy Rameez?' I went pointing up the screen.

'Them Irish ones.'

I paused one moment. Then I goes, 'Make you right Rameez.'

'Four Pernods be sweet Nicky.'

'How's my sis?' Touch of the subtle tactics. If Rameez

was putting it up our Sharon this week his honour made it he was in my debt and he got to buy. On the other hand if he never bothered with it this week then I doshed. And on the occasion he wanted it but Sharon never pushed her boat out then I got serious financial problems.

He gave it thinking.

'Let me see Nicky, maybe I purchase this round after all,' he went.

Javed went up the bar.

'To what does I owes the pleasure of your company?' he carried on. 'Or were you only passing by?'

'I was seeking you,' I goes. Always hard yacking to Rameez without falling into the lingo. 'I was seeking you for an honourable witness.'

'An honourable witness,' he turned round and said. 'An honourable witness.'

He gave some more thinking.

'Nicky my bro,' he went, 'you have fingered the right geezer man. You have come to the most honourable fucking witness in the whole borough like you knows. Carry on please now.'

Javed was back with the drinks. All tipped the new glasses in the old glasses. Javed took the empties back up the bar. They liked a tidy table.

'You heard about the stabbing up the Job Centre Rameez?'

'I heard Nicky. I was not there myself so I did not

observe it personal. I do not myself claim benefits as you knows. It would be immoral as I have a regular income.'

'You pay that income tax in the bargain?'

He clocked me like I was a sudden bad smell came out from under the table. Then he cottoned I was making joke here. 'Ha ha Nicky!' he went. 'Ha ha Nicky!' all his geezers cried. 'Very very funny man!'

'Nah, well, Rameez I was never thinking you were there in person—'

'Although it is true Nicky I am collecting my debtors there occasional.'

Job Shop was always the best spot for collecting. Get your giro in the post but you sign on once a fortnight and everyone knew where you were. Not good when you got creditors. Smart move was transferring your claim to Ilford or Stratford. Compulsory to use the Social Security in your home area but you could sign on up the Job Centre anywhere.

Half the borough owed Rameez. His geezers stood outside Westbury Rd and collected.

'I was present there today Rameez.'

'So I heard Nicky. Must be it was very traumatising.'

'Very traumatising indeed Rameez. You recollect how some stabbings did happen in my past. Now you knows how I trying to go clean, right? Except it is very traumatising how them shaftings they seem to follow me round.'

'You have my sympathy Nicky.'

'Appreciate it. Then maybe you heard how me and Jimmy Foley we was walking up Church Hill after when Jimmy got himself shot.'

'I heard that too Nicky. And I heard you was very nimble and quick and dodged behind Jimmy even when them bullets was flying.'

'As fortune had it Rameez, Jimmy happened to fall between me and them shooters.'

'How I heard it Nicky. Carry on.'

'Well, you can imagine Rameez Old Bill been investigating them twin disasters.'

'Never give a shit I imagine.'

'Well, not quite, matter of fact. They got their forensics in. Took the statements. Something strange going down. Full murder enquiry and then the attempted on Jimmy. Credit where it due, they took it serious even though it was unemployed people.'

'Welfare state Nicky. Every citizen got a right to benefits and a murder enquiry. Nice to see them public servants doing their duty.'

'Yeah. . .'

We sipped our glasses. You never had to go too quick with Rameez. Life got a natural rhythm.

'Now they want me for meeting them up the Village at ten.'

'They do?'

'Yeah.'

'Who do?'

'Them public servants.'

'Them public servants? What for, they buy you a Red Bull?'

'Hoping they buy me several. Only they never turned round and said what for. Only the fuck I knows I needs me a witness there, some geezer I can trust over the honour.'

Rameez looked proud.

'And I asking you Rameez to be my geezer with honour. Geezer what Old Bill respect.'

That started them all cackling, even without the nod off Rameez his boys they all had to start cackling.

'And I got Bridget Tansley off the *Guardian*.'

'Her with that firm little body?'

'Her.'

'Nice move Nicky. She doing anything after?'

'Be going home I reckon same as ever.'

'How I was thinking. She a nice little bird you knows Nicky. Good writing in that paper too. You know how I reckons she may be one very beautiful lover, you hear what I'm saying?' Then he remembered he was putting it up my sis this week. 'In a purely theoretical sense course Nicky. Purely imagination type thing.'

'Course Rameez.'

'You are making this into a very attractive piece of work

Nicky. In fact only one small point is still remaining to trouble me.'

'Lettuce Rameez?'

'Where the lettuce Nicky?'

'Got to be straight with you Rameez, not insult you with financial disrespect. No dosh in this so far. Only your rep as an honourable witness person situation.'

'Hmmm.'

We sat there sipping. All his geezers thinking their thoughts. I often wondered they all thought the same thoughts the same time.

'Nicky Burkett,' went Rameez after suitable interval for reflection.

'Is me.'

'You being a geezer like a white brother.'

'Make me proud Rameez.'

'We take you on trust.'

'Appreciate it brother.'

'Twenty per cent of any earnings you have from this business.'

'Twenty per cent you turned round and said Rameez?'

'Special consideration on account of your attendant sister like.'

'Twenty per cent?'

'Yes Nicky?'

Sensible geezer like yours truly kept his gob shut. Twenty per, maybe a hundred and twenty per, best you never argued. And best you never hid any.

Being as there might be no earners. Only Rameez and me we both knew there was a chance up the Village. One the Old Bill, one some paper. Not the *Guardian* only some shit sheet somewhere.

'Pleasure to do business with you Rameez.'

'Pleasure to do business with you Nicky. We be there for you man. And after you need it. Ten o'clock.'

'Safe Rameez. Appreciate it.'

They carried on sipping. Procedure was after I finished my bit of business I left. So I drank my drink up and I followed procedure.

Noreen told me get home and she'd bring a take-away before we went up the Village.

Tell the truth I was worn out. Could be the trauma. Could be negotiating with Rameez. Could be the fear of Noreen. I went home and went in the bedroom and laid down and got me a nice bit of kip. It was peace. It was quiet. I hoped maybe Noreen forgot and never came for me and TT never followed me and I could stay in and spend my time in the land of nod. I was done.

Then her key came in the door.

'Nicky?'

I never answered.

'Nicky?'

I thought maybe if she never came in the bedroom I

could carry on kipping.

First she went in the kitchen. Things were going on plates. Then she came in.

'Nicky what you doing sleeping there?'

'Only sleeping Noreen.'

'Why?'

'I was tired Noreen.' Sometimes you got to spell things out with birds.

'Why you got no clothes on?'

'I took them off Noreen. For sleeping.'

She smirked. 'You could give me ideas Nicky.'

Oh no. Not them ideas. Ideas meant only one thing.

'Noreen it's my night off innit?' Matter of fact it wasn't Friday but worth a try.

'No it ain't Nicky.'

'And I thought you was punishing me Noreen. Withholding them rights like.'

'Yes Nicky. Only I been thinking after you suffering all that trauma you poor boy, you was telling me about maybe you was in need of having a little loving.' She giggled. 'So I was thinking of putting them conjugals on you after all.'

'Noreen you brought that take-away, know what I mean? We got to gob that then get down the boozer.'

'Mmmm.'

'You got Indian or Chinese?'

'Nicky I'm getting them ideas.'

'Or Sri Lankan? It be getting cold out in that kitchen.'

'I reckon I could eat that take-away right here.'

'Or Caribbean or Turkish or Thai?'

She moved towards me.

'Or Australian?' I went kind of desperate.

'Lie still Nicky.'

'No!'

She went in the kitchen then she came back with one of the plates of grub. She waved on it cooling it down. It smelled Chinese.

'Nicky,' she went very soft and seductive.

'Yes Noreen?' Very quiet and trepidatious.

'You know how they always talk about some geezer or some girl licking honey or chocolate off their lover like?'

'No Noreen. Can't say as I do.'

'All them magazines and that. And films. Very wicked.'

'Ah.' Never knew the right answer here, like a lot of conversations with Noreen it was general best not to go too far in either direction. 'Ah,' I went again.

'You reckon we could do it with mushroom curry?'

One moment I reckoned I misheard. Then I knew I never.

'MUSHROOM CURRY!' I went. 'JESUS!' I was heading for the wardrobe.

'Lie still!'

I did. And I got no clothes on. I was feeling very very vulnerable like.

The best Chinese in Walthamstow was on Markhouse Rd opposite Jimmy's Café. Best café and best Chinese, only reason for going up Markhouse Rd. I smelled their mushroom curry now.

Noreen was waving it about, cooling it down. Very considerate of her.

She started on the belly. She put her plate very close then she tipped it up gentle so mushroom curry rolled all over my belly. This Noreen now, this was your bird worked for BA up the West End. Got computer certificates. Free tickets to Antigua. She got turned on tipping mushroom curry all over a geezer's belly.

'YAAAH!'

I was never screaming on account of the heat. It was only round gas mark three. I was screaming on account of the trauma.

Then she started on smoothing it down all over my privates.

I passed out.

They reckon in a car crash and other severe shock the human body can't take it no more so it goes into unconscious. Like Jimmy Foley when he got shot. Next time I clocked Jimmy we got to talk about it more. Except I never could talk to Jimmy about this. Nor any other geezer. Maybe ten seconds I fainted. Not as long as Jimmy admitted, and not needing major surgery after.

When I woke up she was licking and sucking. And she

got no clothes on in the bargain.

Jesus.

Jesus.

Jesus.

She licked and she sucked. Bits of mushroom so far. And sauce. And trimmings.

'Nicky them bits of beansprouts, they been growing all the time in your short and curlies? They never came in this curry I'm sure.' She chewed them. She giggled atrocious.

When she wiped it round with her tongue it seemed to get hotter.

Sudden I couldn't believe it, it was the most exciting happening since I got my first pint of lager after I came out of nick. It was like West Ham winning away. It was like getting a giro they never owed you.

'YAAAH!' I cried out again. Only different reasons this time.

'YAAAH!' she cried out in the bargain. We were away.

We forgot all about the rice. It stayed on the plate. She cleared up all the curry nice and clean off me.

'Now my turn Noreen,' I went. 'Reckon there's still some curry left on the plate.'

'No.'

'I'm hungry.'

'You have to wait.'

'I can't.'

'Yes you can.'

'You never heard about that equality Noreen?'

'Next time.'

'Getting cold that curry Noreen. Know how that monosodium glutamate gets all stodgy? You want me to be having a little taster round you we better be doing it quick.'

No answer. Except sudden she pushed me back flat and she climbed up on top of me and whoosh she was never taking no for an answer and we were doing it like normal people and it was unbelievable and there it all was.

She lay down on me and she was laughing laughing.

So was I.

'Oh Nicky,' she sighed.

I just sighed. Seemed to be the move.

I was hungry no doubting now. But I thought it was best off the plate.

'Noreen we got to get up the boozer.'

She only giggled.

'Noreen you want your rice now? You had enough to eat?'

She only giggled.

Then she rolled off me and she lay on her back and we both giggled something stupid.

'Reckon I get in the shower first Nicky, all right?'

I got the curry on me. She got the shower first. How the world was set up.

'No problem Noreen.'

She went off. I did get a little more snooze after all.

Then I heated up the rest of the curry and we had a nice cup of tea. Then we went up the boozer for meeting TT and O'Malley.

SIX

THE VILLAGE WAS JUMPING.

Least it was fidgeting. Packed as usual, only no
action worth the mention. Even when they were trying to
pull some bird it took them four hours yacking. By the time
they finished they forgot what they started out for.
Accounted for not many babies born round the middle
classes.

TT and O'Malley and a thin suspicious-looking geezer
got to be the DI were sitting in the corner.

Bridget propping up the bar ordering a coke.

Noreen and me we made our entrance. Punters up the
Village they never reckoned me at all, least when they did

they preferred not. Noreen though they all knew Noreen. Either her badminton group or her mum's line dancing or her evening classes or her school mates off the Internet or her dad's football coaching or just on account of she was the tastiest fucking bird in the whole borough. They all wanted to know Noreen.

We fought our way through. Not exactly that quiet chat Old Bill was wanting.

'Pint of lager TT,' I went. 'And none of that fucking German real ale fucking lager, know what I mean?' You could tell all the real ale drinkers round there. Made them grow beards. 'And a shandy for Noreen.'

'Gin and tonic please,' went Noreen. 'Ice and lemon.'

'You know DS O'Malley,' goes TT. 'And this is Detective Inspector Finlay. He is responsible for ethnics.'

He made it sound like cleaning the drains.

'Pleased to meet you,' went Noreen. 'Ethics, Mr Finlay?'

'Ethics? We ain't got none of those,' he went cackling. 'Ethnics. Asylums. Imports. All that. And more specific, crime by ethnics. Illegal immigrants. Contraband. Cigs and alcohol. Housing Benefit. All that.'

'Oh all that.' I bought my contraband the same as everyone else. No point paying four times in the offie what you paid on the street. Old Bill did the same. Except they never bought them. And I never saw difference between asylums and anyone else for committing our crimes. Still, got to keep Old Bill busy.

'Bit noisy in here,' went Finlay. 'We go out in the garden or what?'

The Village got a garden out the back. Nice for sipping your booze on a quiet sunny evening. Only problem was now it was shivering cold in winter and talking about rain.

'You make it worth my while?' I turned round and said. 'Catching pneumonia?'

'Come out in the garden Nicky.'

'I got my witnesses with me?'

'You what?'

'I got my witnesses.'

'What fucking witnesses?'

'Just on account of I got turned over too many fucking times off Old Bill.'

Finlay gave TT a butcher's. Then he gave O'Malley another butcher's. Then up walked Bridget from the bar. 'This here's my first witness,' I went. 'Ms Tansley off the *Walthamstow Guardian*.'

'You must be fucking joking,' went Finlay.

'Never more serious. And Noreen course except she's more like my bird not witness as such.'

'Partner Nicky.'

'Same difference Noreen.'

'You must be fucking joking.'

'You already turned round and said that mister.'

'Off the fucking rag?'

'Good evening Inspector,' goes Bridget. Knew him already.

'She my witness. Trust Bridget absolutely on the confidentials. You never want it spread, she's your bird.'

'Woman Nicky.'

'Generally up till two weeks. Bridget hold everything up to two weeks depending on circumstances. Two weeks then she splatters it. Excepting a few things you never can trust her on, then she splatters it straight off, am I right Bridget?'

'Well, big sex stories and runners we can sell to the nationals, Nicky, you've got to make exceptions.'

'You get the picture mister? Know where you stand? Most of Old Bill on the take off the papers anyhow, what the problem?'

'Fucking *Walthamstow Guardian*. Fucking cheap tight bastards . . .'

Now we all knew the problem. He never got any backhanders off the *Guardian*. Tabloids you could expect a little earner. Locals were more or less straight.

Then in walked Rameez and his boys.

Boozer went quiet.

Rameez and Aftab and Afzal and Javed. Dressed for the night. Shiny suits and big long coats. Only bits missing were their holsters.

Rameez waved Aftab to one corner. Afzal another. Javed came and stood three paces after Rameez, then went in the corner. Best of all Rameez might prefer a staircase so he could come down the middle. He spent the afternoon watching old westerns out the classics section up the video shop on Hoe St.

'Second witness,' I goes to DI Finlay. 'Neighbourhood watch.'

'Jesus H. Christ,' he goes.

'More like Mohammed than Jesus you want to be technical.'

'You want the whole bleeding borough hearing our business? What the fuck you want a witness for anyhow, this ain't no official interview and you don't even know what I want you for yet?'

'Exactly. Only whatever the fuck it is I want a fucking witness, you hear what I'm saying?'

'Jesus H. Christ.'

'I'm sorry Inspector,' goes TT. 'Little bastard's a nasty little bastard.'

'We go out in the garden,' went Finlay. He took his pint and he went out the back.

'I'm sorry Nicky,' goes TT. 'Fucking bastard's a nasty fucking bastard.' Then he followed him.

O'Malley only shrugged. Went after.

We all copped a few glances round each other. 'Very friendly geezer,' went Rameez. 'Definitely failed on the public liaison course,' Bridget turned round and said. Noreen got no comment. We all went outside where the filth already sat down by a table with a sunshade. We pulled up chairs and benches and we waited for it.

Soon as we parked it started raining. We carried on sitting. We heard what the DI got to turn round and say.

'You being the victim,' went Finlay. 'We got a new victim policy. Keep them informed. Public service duty like.'

We all clocked each other. Rameez he started cackling straight off. Bridget she gave it a moment then she giggled. Me and Noreen we waited for later when we could spread it round the borough.

'Yeah and my mum's standing for queen,' I goes.

'And I celebrating Christmas this year,' goes Rameez.

Victims rated about as high on the Old Bill clapometer as a cheese and pickle sandwich. Something you got into when there was nothing else on the menu.

'Only Nicky he weren't never the victim innit?' went Noreen.

'Hold on up Noreen,' I turned round and said. 'You forgetting that trauma? First I got to witness a gouging. Then my best mate Jimmy Foley he got shot three times stood next to me. I be putting in my claim up the Criminal Injuries Compensation Board first thing Monday. Deeply affected. Unable to go to work. Loss of earnings. Personal distress. And Old Bill be my evidence for that disability allowance in the bargain. And no need to sign on for that Noreen. All legit.'

'Shut the fuck up,' goes Finlay.

'No need to be rude.'

'You try that one for starters. More to the point they'll be coming after you. You're the witness. They don't know if your mate pulls through or not, so they don't know if he's a witness to the murder. They don't know if you clocked them when your mate got shot. What they do know is, maybe you saw them both times.'

''Scuse me,' goes Rameez.

'What?'

''Scuse me if I ask so bleedin' what? He get visible and maybe they got to do something. Till then they keep their Judge Dreads down, know what I mean? Witness interference, dodgy game mate. You never do it only when strictly necessary, you get me?' Rameez like he was an expert on witness interference.

'Yeah.'

'Yeah?'

'Yeah. Only we want Nicky here to make it his business. We want him to go after them. Show himself.'

There was a little sigh round the garden like a Scouser came in or we witnessed a miracle.

'How much?' I went.

'You see,' went Finlay. 'They were Lithuanians.'

SEVEN

'WHAT?'
　　　'Where?'
'Whosit?'
'Lithuanians,' he went again.
'Jesus, I reckoned they were straight.'
'We got his ID off the victim. Never found his passport but we found enough. Basanavicius.'
'Come again?'
'B-A-S-A-N-A-V-I-C-I-U-S.'
'You sure he weren't a Geordie?'
'Jonas Basanavicius.'
'How you spell Jonas?' I went.

'Why he was by you up the Job Centre. He was under the name Beasant. Changed his name. Started with a B. Signed on the same day as you.'

I never got any luck.

'So why he changed his name?' I goes. 'Computer never cope or what?'

'He was a grass Nicky.'

'He what?'

'Police up Edmonton were using him as a grass. Changed his ID. Gave him a name. Same initials. John Beasant.'

The fuck were they telling me all this, even when they wanted me involved?

'This thing is wider than Walthamstow Nicky,' he went. 'This thing is large.'

We went marching up and down the street. Me and Noreen. Up to the corner by Beulah Rd where they got the alcohol centre, handy so you could get straight in the boozer after your AA meeting. Back again. Then up again carrying on up Walthamstow Village proper where it went all quiet at night, museums and whatnot. First time I went up there since we went on a school trip. Back again. Past the boozer again and on all the way to Hoe St. Turned right, heading for the Central and bought a packet of gathia up the Asian shops. Chewed on them all the way back. Noreen yacking. All the rest still up the garden while we took a stroll and quietly discussed the issues.

'Nicky the fuck you think you're doing?'

'What Noreen?'

'The fuck you even hesitating about on their fucking offer?'

Now you got to tread very careful round Noreen. Sometimes you reckoned she reckoned one thing and it turned out total opposite. Sometimes you be sure you gave the right answer, then it turned out you dropped a big one. Trouble with women you never could get it right. So for starters I was never sure which way she was upset. I ought to be taking their offer or I ought never even thinking about it?

'Noreen,' I interrupted eventual.

'Grrr,' she went.

''Scuse me one moment.'

'You saying something Nicky? You finally saying something?' Leaving aside she never stopped one moment for me to speak. 'It better be the right answer my friend I'm telling you.'

''Scuse me Noreen I ask you one question?'

'One question yeah. Better be quick too.'

'You want me taking their dosh or what?'

Whack.

I got it wrong.

She packed a mean smack you got to hand it to Noreen. I got so many black eyes off her I was like the man who

61

walked into doors. Fortunate I was a non-violent person, one in a household was enough. Times I tried to tell her you could always work things out with sensible verbals, no need for that violence. Only with Noreen sensible verbals got their limits. When their limits were up I got a whacking.

I stemmed the blood coming out my hooter. 'So you reckon I never take their dosh? Keep away from crime like altogether?'

'Jesus Nicky. Well fucking done! Pass your GCSE in staying clean! Pity you had to take a bleeding re-sit! Only remember you aren't never a criminal no more now you living with me, you got me?'

'Hear what you're saying Noreen. Only one moment I reckoned maybe on account of helping Old Bill, clean up the streets and that, and seeing how it was easy dosh for not doing fuck all, maybe you give me the go-ahead just one time innit?'

'Not doing fuck all?'

'Well Noreen they give me the notes first, then I sit at home and do fuck all, how I clocked it. They never ask for their notes back, know what I mean?'

'Oh yeah?'

'Well . . .'

'Yeah and give me a few wells. So you never do nothing only sit at home so you think they sit there happy? Or you think they start to get aerated so they nick you on some piece of rubbish they dream up, Going Equipped or Obstruct Police or Offensive Weapon, am I right, so you plead not guilty and they got half a bleeding dozen Old Bill witnesses and you going to get a not guilty? Make me laugh Nicky, am I right?'

'Noreen you got a point have to admit.'

'So you back in the courts or maybe they get you doing something up Edmonton after all what we don't even know about yet, and they drop all them charges sudden?'

'See what you're saying Noreen.'

We were sitting by the bus stop on Hoe St now. She was shaking with her anger. I was shaking with whatsits. Or maybe we were cold, anyhow we were shaking. I reckoned now was the time.

'Only Noreen I got to do something,' I went.

'What? Don't give me no more rubbish Nicky.'

'Got to show you a bit Noreen. Don't know what it is, only maybe we take a butcher's before we make my final decision like.'

'What?'

I took out the package I got off the geezer up the Job Shop when he got shafted. I still got it in my strides.

'Noreen, when he got stabbed, that geezer he turned round and he gave me this personal like.'

'What?'

'And he turned round and went "Elena" before he croaked.'

63

'What?'

'Thassit.'

'Nicky what you telling me here?'

'Just told you Noreen.'

'You telling me when this geezer got stabbed he gave you this package and he turned round and said "Elena"?'

'I believe that's what I just turned round and said Noreen.'

'You telling me this?'

Even for a woman this was getting boring. Why their conversations went on so long. Still best for a quiet life. 'Telling you this Noreen.'

'You got this package all this time?'

'Yeah.'

'And you never tell Old Bill?'

'Course not. Privileged information like. Geezer wanted to tell Old Bill he tell them himself.'

'Except he was dead.'

'Granted Noreen, take your point. Only I reckon he was wanting me to give this package to this Elena. Kind of personal. Last wish type of thing.'

'Jesus Nicky. And you never open it yet?'

'Want to show it to you first Noreen. You being my bird.'

'Partner.'

'You first before Old Bill course Noreen. You being special.'

She started leaking.

You always got round them eventual. And it being a dead geezer and a bird's name. Sentimental.

Tears running now.

'Oh Nicky . . .'

'No need to get carried off Noreen . . .'

'Never thought you had it in you Nicky, sometimes you do surprise me I got to admit.'

'Nah . . .' I went modest. 'Any geezer do the same Noreen.'

'But you did it.'

'True words Noreen. So you understand I got to be seeing what Old Bill want to be telling. Before I open the parcel and found out about this Elena like. If she in there.'

'See what you're saying Nicky. Only being as I'm more important to you right now, I'm thinking we better take a butcher's at your package innit?'

Nosy little bleeder in fact.

EIGHT

IT WAS TIED UP with string, not too big. Just fit in your sky rocket. When you shook it you got a little rattling. Outside was brown paper, then when you took it off there was a little Jiffy bag. We tore that open. Inside was more wrapping. We took that off.

Then there was a necklace sparkling shiny.

Delicate. Silver. Jewels. Came out of the east.

'Jesus,' went Noreen.

'Jesus,' I goes.

'For Elena,' she goes.

'Cost a fortune,' I goes. 'Got murdered for it.'

'Came off the market,' she goes.

'What?'

'Came off the market. Very pretty Nicky and that only it worth about a fiver. Show you the stall when you want.'

'Shit. So he never loved her a lot.'

'No telling Nicky. Can't measure love in terms of diamonds, am I right?'

'Oh, er, course Noreen. Love you never can measure it.'

'So they never kill him for it Nicky.'

'Unless she was some other geezer's missis he was giving a necklace to.'

'True Nicky.'

Only there was something else in the Jiffy bag when we took the wrapping out. Noreen put her hand in.

It was his passport.

Noreen picked it out. She laid it on her mitt and she stared at it. Jonas Basanavicius. All it said. Unfortunate no matter how hard Noreen clocked it it never spoke any more.

'It's his passport,' I went.

'True Nicky.'

'You reckon he gave me the parcel on account of the necklace?' I went. 'Or on account of the passport?'

'I dunno Nicky.'

'Or both?'

'I dunno Nicky.'

'There got to be an answer.'

Trouble was we got no idea what it was. We sat there stumped.

Then Noreen picked up the brown paper kind of casual. We both clocked it the same time.

Kind of made me feel like I was stupid. It got an address on it. Where they were supposed to be. Only no stamps. Maybe it was for personal delivery.

It went:

ELENA BASANAVICIUS
UZUPIO 18 – 9
VILNIUS

Ten seconds or more me and Noreen we clocked each other straight up. Then we turned.

'We go back and we see what they got to say,' Noreen went.

I never knew what we decided but it seemed we decided something. It was very handy I got to admit. I was going to deal with Old Bill anyhow. Good if Noreen agreed though. Unfortunate if she never agreed, have to do it on the sly. Now I got official permission for it. Least for talking.

Reason I was going to do it, I reckoned they were offering big ones.

We went back up the Village. I was kind of frozen stiff by now, not looking forward to sitting out in their garden.

'Noreen,' went the bird behind the bar, 'your friends went up the Italian.'

'All of them?'

'Them four Asian lads and the girl off the paper and them three looked like CID.'

'Thanks.'

We had to be wondering how their conversation was flowing, Rameez and the DI. We went back the few doors to the Italian gaff. Only one time before I went in there when I never had the chance to avoid it. The arties went there. Good atmosphere bad nosh, suit them nicely. Get a better pizza off the take-away down the bottom of the market. Even better you get a curry.

In the Italian gaff they were stuck round the corner in an alcove. When we walked in every geezer as usual copped a brisk one round Noreen's business area. Not my fault I got a classy bird so I never took notice. We went round where they sat on a long table the eight of them. They kept us places.

What they were gassing on, they were yacking nostalgic about old villains. In the good old days.

Kind of geezers Rameez looked up to when he was starting out. Geezers the DI was nicking when he was DC. Like Jimmy The Gob O'Neill and Henry The Blade Fairweather and Mervyn Gold Boy Copthorpe. They were going back so far they were in short knickers. Villains did bank raids. Drugs were still dear. Kids nicked Fords. Listening to them was like clocking an old video.

Bridget was taking notes for the Lost Memories page.

'Remember how they culled that security guard, never even knew there was CCTV?'

'Jesus, no-one heard of CCTV! First place on the manor got it!'

'And you heard how that time they blew the safe up Thomas Cook's, all they got was Turkish lira!'

'Had to go up Turkey to spend it!'

'And remember Rats Waller how he went up Casualty after his difference with Henry The Blade? Got a metal went in him the front, came out just showing out the back?'

'Walked in Casualty himself. Missed everything.'

'Henry meant it that way. Knew every body part did Henry. Only wanting for teaching Rats a lesson.'

'Mind his manners.'

'And Ashok Mahmood?'

'Ah, Ashok . . .'

They shook their bonces wondering.

'How Ashok robbed every bank in Walthamstow the same day? When they went up the first one after him he was in the next. Six banks. Never fussed with building societies. What a pro . . .'

'Took the notes and out of the country by teatime. Never came back. Up Sharjah some place.'

'Only his mate doing a fifteen up Whitemoor for conspiracy.'

'Supplied the shooter.'

'All the shooters. Six he was carrying.'

'Them were the days.'

''Scuse me,' went Noreen.

'Yeah?'

'You ordered or you too busy?'

'Yeah we ordered. And we ordered for you.'

'Very considerate. Any idea what you ordered for us?'

'Margheritas.'

'Eat or drink?' I goes.

'And garlic bread. Keep the devil away.'

'You better go now then.'

'Very fucking funny.' He sipped his Scotch. He was trying to be cool, wait till later for checking out his offer. Only he never could wait. 'You do the right thing then?' he went.

'How much?'

'You want me spelling it out in here?'

'Yeah.'

'Big one. We could make it a big one. For the right result.'

'You making joke innit?'

'Pretty fucking generous. What the fuck you want?'

'Three big ones for starters. Up front. Here. On the table.'

'What?'

'Then one more for every villain you lift.'

'Fucking and the rest! The fuck you on about? I could

get them hit for that much, save the taxpayer's money.'

'Choice is yours mate. Only remember we got witnesses. You want co-operation, endanger my life, do all the hard work for you, only remember you made the offer and I got six pairs of mince pies clocking you.'

'Fuck you Burkett!'

'No skin off my hooter. Me, I'm for a quiet life. Sit in my gaff. Watch videos. Take drugs.'

Then the nosh came. Being as it was on expenses the pigs all ordered the dearest on the menu for themselves. Rameez got pasta, heard it strengthened your slicing arm. His boys got veggie pizzas, never trusted the Italians with meat. Everyone got wine. The charge probably went up the police accountant for a feast with councillors on some clean up the streets. We ate up.

Just before the pudding came the DI pulled out his paper.

All he turned round and said was 'Fuck you.'

Then he counted it out in fifties. Sixty of them.

All the time he got the dosh with him. Only wanted to see he could get me on the cheap.

I put it in my back one.

'Now you want to turn round and tell me what the fuck this is all about?' I asked him.

NINE

'YOU SEE NICKY,' goes the DI all friendly, like I was the back leg of a cockroach.

'Like a fucking carrot,' I goes.

'Eh?' he goes.

'Yeah,' I goes.

'Oh,' he goes.

Then he starts again.

'You see Nicky,' he goes.

'Like a fucking carrot,' I goes.

This time he carries on.

'This thing is wider than Walthamstow.'

Then he sits back for applause. Maybe forgets we heard

it before. Not being put off by the silence, he carries on ploughing.

'And wider than Edmonton too,' he goes.

'Pretty fucking wide,' I turns round and says.

'These Lithuanians . . .'

'Coming from Lithuania,' goes TT.

O'Malley rolls his mincers.

'When they were operating in Lithuania, which is the other side of Poland—'

'And before Pakistan—' goes Rameez.

'They were into it. Import-export, drugs, extortion, car sales, rock concerts, they controlled all the channels.'

'Remote,' goes TT.

'The fuck you talking about TT?' he goes. Then he carries on. 'You wanted to move in Lithuania, you wanted to import a motor, you wanted to start a restaurant, you got to shell the right people.'

'Course.'

'Government, politicians, officials, police, gangsters. All in it together.'

'Like here innit?'

Only he never found that amusing. 'But that was when it was all under the Russians. Then it all started to go wrong.'

'Politics again.'

'Two things went wrong. First the government went, the Russians in charge. Then all the rest went, the Russians who controlled the system. So you got no system.'

'Got to have a system.'

'Second the gangsters all started fighting each other.'

'Terrible waste of resources,' goes Rameez.

'Too much competition. With no system you got new people coming in, you got gangsters from Russia trying to expand, you got the Italians, you got new business start-ups wanting a piece, there was no end to it. Too many snakes in one cabbage patch, say no more.'

'Say no more.'

'They started murdering each other. And some of them they had to get out.'

'Needless.'

'Like our friend Basanavicius.'

'Jonas to his mates.'

'Jonas. And more. They came to Britain.'

'And do a bit of work while they're about it.'

'Exactly. Came on a tourist visa. Only then they made it a working holiday. Started small. Smashing motors, bit of protection, retailing Es at clubs.'

'Small. Good bit of work but small.'

'Only what they were really after was moving in other people's yards.'

'Snakes in them yards.'

'Yeah.'

'Soon be no cabbages to go round, know what I mean?'

'See, these Lithuanians, they ain't like our villains. How they work, they ain't got no real subtlety.'

'You got to be subtle,' goes Rameez.

'They start in their own community. They goes up to some Lithuanian merchant, rich geezer, some legit import export or clothing bandit or corner shop or banker and they take his motor.'

'Fair enough.'

'They take his Merc, they all got Mercs, then they turn round and say unless he doshes them ten thousand notes he don't get his Merc back.'

'He goes to Old Bill?'

'Then they turn round and say he goes to Old Bill they whack him.'

I could clock Rameez's brain going eighty-five to the dozen.

'Not very subtle,' he goes giggling, thinking up ideas.

'So they get a kind of grounding in the Lithuanian community, then natural they want to expand their business.'

'Get a government grant.'

'First they hit the Greeks.'

'Nah.'

'Then the Turks.'

'Nah.'

'Even the Jamaicans. They stopped short of the North London Brits so far. Them from Islington. Too big.'

'Too nasty.' Gave me a shiver even thinking of it.

'But they started very very large turf wars. Taking over

club protection. Already three shootings in Clapton. Buying up motor dealers – least, borrowing them over. Internet cafés, all theirs now. Snack bars. Shootings everywhere. Where there's cash, they're interested.'

'In control.'

'Nearly.'

'Except you got a grass.'

'Edmonton boys got a grass. Already they lifted a few villains. Some of them top nickings, major faces.'

'But they get cross.'

'He was a chancer. Could have left. But he was earning from the game, then he was getting even more for his grassing. He knew there was grief around.'

'Jesus. All that dosh and still he was signing on.'

'For appearances. When it got hot he moved out of Edmonton and he gave up on the villainy. Living in Stratford. Still he wanted to get a giro coming, case the neighbours wondered how he lived. Only he never wanted to sign on local. So he came to Walthamstow.'

'Not getting no giro no more.'

'They found him.'

'And now you got no grass.'

'Edmonton got no grass. So they want to find a new lead to their boys. And they asked us to help. Knew we got witnesses.'

'Where all that dosh came from.'

'Like you know Nicky, we never got this kind of dosh

up Chingford. This kind of notes, got to be regional. Organised Crime Squad.'

'Course.'

'So they wanted a lead like I said. Someone these villains already got marked so they reckon it's legit. Let them know you wanting to do a deal. Show yourself.'

'You thought of Jimmy Foley?' I went.

He gave a kind of a snort.

'We thought of you Nicky. All you got to do is show yourself. We give you the names, you go up Edmonton and make a few like enquiries. Pop in a couple of businesses, mention you want to come to an agreement. We move you out to a safe house. Then we await developments.'

Developments like me getting the fuck out of there soon as I was out of sight.

We came out the eatery all feeling kind of pleased.

I got three big ones.

Rameez get his commission later.

Finlay did a deal, tell his gaffers.

TT probably stepped up the ladder.

O'Malley got a night out from his missis.

Bridget got a story waiting.

All of us got a free meal. We were mellow.

So none of us was ready for DI Finlay getting whacked over the bonce with iron bars by four Lithuanian gangsters.

Noreen and me, we just crossed over Orford Rd heading

for West Avenue to get home. Rameez and his boys stayed on the same side of Orford Rd going back up Hoe St, do some collecting. Rameez got his motor there too. Bridget unlocking her pushbike just getting on. Old Bill though they parked up in the village. They just headed for their motor, maybe pop in the boozer first then do a bit of drink driving back up the station.

So we were split up when the Lithuanians had it with Finlay's skull.

I was feeling up my money. Maybe put it in the post office. Maybe start a small business like they always told you in the nick, fucking silliest idea I ever heard. Or maybe I have a week of drink and drugs and casual sex.

We clocked a crack like nothing quite like I ever heard. Not a motor crash on one hand. Not a twig snapping on the other. Not a door slamming. Not a jaw breaking. More a big whump first and then a little whimp after.

It was an iron bar landing on DI Finlay. Several iron bars only one special one landing on his Judge Dread.

Then they were gone.

They got a motor in the middle of the road, driver waiting. It was a big Volvo, got no plates. They were in it and away. Up Hoe St. No fucking use TT getting on his mobile or his radio or whatever the fuck he had.

Finlay was down. He was mash up.

We stood there gawping. These were serious geezers. Fucking kill a copper.

We all went back and stood there while O'Malley got an ambulance.

'He dead?'

'Fuck.'

He got a dent in the side of his skull. No telling he was dead or not. He was never doing any line dancing.

And his arm was bent back funny and he got blood on his lug and drool coming out his gob.

'Jesus.'

'Fuck.'

'Nicky,' went Rameez.

'Yeah?'

'They never wanted you. You the witness only they never wanted you.'

'Nah.'

'So they never know you the witness. Even though you with Jimmy up the job shop.'

'Maybe.'

'Or they never care. Want the DI.'

'Yeah.'

'They reckon he threaten their firm?'

'Yeah.'

'Or maybe he on the backhand? Only he never deliver?'

'Yeah.'

'Or he working some rival firm?'

'Yeah.' I never gave a fuck. I clocked some things in my time only I never clocked like this.

'Don't any of you leave,' went TT. Always good on the procedures was TT. Like any of us looked like leaving.

It was getting very kind of samey though being a witness to murder. One murder up the job shop, one attempted on Jimmy Foley and now one could be either when it panned out.

I was vex. More to the point I was shitless. All well and good Rameez reckoning they were never after me. The way things were going they could get me by accident or they might slice me in bits on account of I looked at them funny or breathed heavy.

We stood there the lot of us about two minutes while twenty Old Bill and four ambulances came on the scene. Attacks on inspectors brought emergency services in numbers. Kind of surprising they never turned out the fire brigade in the bargain. Hose old Finlay down.

They turned the boozer into a temporary incident room. Fucked all the punters off out. Meant they could take all the witness statements and down a few freeman's the same time.

Noreen and me, what we knew you could write on the back of a giro. Few geezers plus the driver we clocked in the motor was all. Speeding up Orford Rd. Wearing balaclavas.

How I rated it was, geezers got a very, very bad attitude.

Noreen she agreed. Not often that happened so I got to make the most of it.

We got home about three. I put the folding in a bag in the freezer. One piece of lady luck, after a crack like that Finlay more than likely forgot he doshed it.

If he never croaked that is.

'Noreen,' I went when we got in and put the kettle on, 'you fancying a touch of howsyourfather?'

'What?'

'Piece of the other? Help us nod off to sleep like?'

'Nicky? You serious?'

'Never more.'

'Nicky it crossed your mind some geezer maybe just got murdered?'

'Yeah.' I put my mitt up her skirt from behind.

'Jesus Nicky. You ain't got no respect at all or what?'

'Noreen you never heard how when someone dies all them others they get that primitive like urge to propriate?'

'What?'

'Like making babies?'

'Nicky you mean procreate?'

'The one.' I got my mitt right between her legs now and massaging. Feel her warm.

'Nicky fuck's sake you wanting a baby?'

'Fuck no! I only got the urge Noreen not got stupid.'

'Jesus Nicky you are so fucking tasteless . . .'

'Yeah . . .'

She was starting to move. She started backing into me.

'Noreen I take you over the worktop here.'

'Don't you bleeding dare.' She hated a mess on her worktop did Noreen. Except it was generally my worktop.

She was panting. So was I.

'Please . . .'

Supposed to be the bird saying please when we got this far. Only it was me.

'Oh all right . . .'

We never ever did it with our clothes on. We always got proper undressed.

Until now.

Fortunate she never got tights on. I pulled her knickers down.

Then we did the business faster than a cat jumping on a budgie. Fact we did it a bit like that. Only thing I ever clocked faster was a prison doctor on speed.

We pulled up our gear again.

'Jesus Nicky,' she went. She giggled. She looked round at the worktop. 'How'd we get up there Nicky? You standing on a chair or what?'

'Superhuman powers Noreen.'

She giggled and blushed and cackled out loud.

She went off up the bathroom for a clean up and I carried on putting the kettle on.

TEN

NEXT MORNING Noreen was off for work and I was out for a paper when my mobile went.

As a rule I never carried my mobile with me when I went out. Last thing I wanted was someone getting hold of me. Just now though it seemed like I ought to be in touch with events so I took it out for an airing.

Except it was never events. It was Mum. And I never clocked the number so I never went unobtainable.

'Nicky!'

I kept quiet.

'Nicky you there?'

'Mmm . . .'

'You by the market?'

Jesus, how the fuck she knew? I took a butcher's all round, never checked her. Still no getting away from her it seemed like.

'You round by that market or what Nicky?'

'Where you Mum?'

'Back indoors what d'you expect? Nicky you get me a bag of rice you hear?'

'Whyn't you get it off Asif?'

'And them cheap bananas five pounds for a pound and some of them red spuds and a cabbage and onions and peanuts and a jigsaw. And a pizza out of Kwiksave.'

'Queen calling or what?'

'Get them things up here Nicky.'

'Very busy geezer Mum.'

'Yeah unemployed very busy, get yourself up here.'

'Got the cleaning to do and the cooking and reading the paper.'

She gave a snort. I switched off. Another peaceful day fucked.

When Food Giant was up the precinct you knew how life was. Cereals in their place, beans in their place. Pizza in another. Cheap too but it got quality. Beans were second to none. Reduced sugar and salt and none of that fucking saccharine gave you cancer. So Noreen reckoned anyhow. Cheap milk. Molasses sugar Noreen's mum and dad reckoned was like what they got in Antigua when they still grew sugar there. Quality booze, believe it. Then they got the best pizzas in the borough.

I bought my paper then instead of turning for home and a read and a nice cup like I deserved I headed up the market and the precinct. Mum somehow reckoned I lived by the market. Fact was I lived ten minutes from the market and she lived thirteen. She reckoned thirteen minutes was unlucky. No sense arguing.

I stopped up the bookshop. Never wanted anything only wanted to look up the birds reading. There were a few nice ones so I hung around. Thought about buying Noreen a present out of my new dosh. No sense buying Mum a book, might as well buy her a ground to air missile. Little Danny though he was another case and getting big so I bought him a true crime. I went out and round a few Caribbean grocers, all kept by Asians. They reckoned they got stalls in seventeen languages up our market. Plus Walthamstow language.

Then a message came on the mobile. Going from bad to worse this was.

'Chingford nick twelve o'clock,' it went. 'TT.'

I went in the Calypso and got a coffee. Two choices for TT. Either tell him to fuck right off or tell him something different. Always best not ignoring Old Bill total so I messaged him back.

'My mum's,' I went. 'Four o'clock.'

I bought some of the necessaries for Mum then I headed

back for the bus station to go visiting Jimmy up Whipps Cross. On the way I looked in the job shop.

Hard to credit it was only yesterday since everything went down. Now it looked kind of peaceful. I wanted information though and there was one person might give it over. Louise Bedworth.

Late in the morning it was getting quieter. They did their bit knocking half the geezers off the dole and getting the other half on training courses to drive forklifts, always the same so their mates in the training schemes made a few bob and no-one ever found work. They were relaxing before doing the hatchet on a few more punters in the afternoon. Louise got one geezer with her so I sat polite till he went.

'All right Louise?' I goes then.

'Jesus. Nicky Burkett. The fuck you doing here not on your signing on day? Don't tell me you came after a job.'

'Came to chat you Louise. Old times good times, all that. Since I turned round and clocked you yesterday I reckoned you might like to sit down and yack a few minutes about the best days of our lives and all that.'

'What?'

'Up McEntee you knows.'

'McEntee?'

'All them French lessons.'

'Jesus Nicky, you reckon them were the best times of my life?'

'And round Wayne Sapsford's that night when his mum was away and you and me, like, you remember in that cupboard?'

'Yeah I remember Nicky. I remember it weren't hardly worth remembering as well. Gone in a fucking flash. Streak of lightning be quicker. And then least you get a bit of thunder after.'

'Ah well Louise we was young then we was only fourteen.'

'Just 'cause I was young Nicky don't mean I wanted to hear goodbye before I heard hello, you get my meaning?'

'Well, maybe it was only me was young Louise. Only I always had fondest memories of you, you hear what I'm saying? Lost love type of thing?'

'Nicky you so full of shit you should spread it on an allotment. The fuck you want?'

'Louise you supposed to talk like that to the public? Might be I came in here after one of them dot com millionaire jobs what all went bust.'

She made a rude noise.

'Or street cleaning operative.'

'Nicky what the fuck you want?'

Louise was kind of a big stocky blonde bird bursting. When she was fourteen she was a good build. Threw the discus and did netball for the school. Now though she kind of got her puppy fat second time round. Being charitable I might give her one if she begged me. Not that she was showing signs of begging.

'Louise you remember that geezer got shafted here yesterday?'

'Yes I do believe I still got that in my recall. Not being so used to murders as some people I do believe I remember him dropping down dead in front of me so I probably won't sleep about twenty years.'

'Very shocking Louise. Traumatising. You and me both.'

'What?'

'I was very sorry you were put through that Louise.'

'?'

'Me, I was going to shaft some geezer, have it where members of the public they never got to suffer that distress. I bet you never got no sleep at all last night. Maybe you even need a comforter some time . . .'

'No fucking chance mate. Not some new one anyhow. I got my kid.'

So she got herself a baby. Accounted for her putting on weight maybe.

'Louise very happy to hear you got in the fambly way. I hope you are truly fulfilled as a female type. Now Louise I was wondering you could tell me all about Mr Beasant.'

'Who?'

'Geezer got stabbed. A few personal details like?'

'What?'

'So I could visit nearest and dearest, offer my condolences and that?'

'Nicky you mad?'

'Least I can do.'

'You think I can give out that kind of information?'

I passed over a fifty.

'For fifty fucking quid?' Only she turned round and said it a lot quieter.

Gave her another of Finlay's fifties.

She put them in her bag sharp. And played with her computer. Not looking at me. Like it seemed she was gazing elsewhere even yacking to some other geezer.

'Nicky I can't give you a printout,' she went. 'They got a record of me then.'

'Read it.'

She clocked her screen. Read it out. I wrote it down.

'John Beasant. Unemployed nine months. Don't believe that, just for the stats. Driver. No HGV licence. And mechanic. Address in Stratford. Signs on here, don't know why. No more info. Almost blank. Never seen one like it.'

'Address?'

'Flat 1, 4 Bolt St, Stratford.'

'Thank you Louise. Anything else?'

'Yeah. Get the fuck out of here.'

'Fancy meeting up later? Finish what we started?'

She clocked me like I was a two-headed Geordie. 'Finish what you started? Mister you finished what you started about one second after you started it. Just piss off.'

'Older now Louise. Considerate of a woman's needs and all that.'

'You ain't being considerate of this one thank you. Out.'

'Thank you for your assistance Louise. I shall always know where to come for career advice.'

She made another rude noise and I turned to go.

Except there were geezers in the doorway and they got shooters.

Now round our way we never got heavy duty shooters. We got geezers with an attitude, right, and we got mean geezers. Now and then these geezers they were feeling they got to whack geezers. Only how they reckoned it, what you couldn't do with a sawnoff wasn't never hardly worth doing. It was true how more recent we got the Yardies with their handguns. Not called for, the way most people clocked it. Even so, given you were going to use a shooter, one thing for sure was you never needed a fucking Kalashnikov. Dead and you were dead. How far the holes went in wasn't hardly to the point.

These Lithuanians got armoury like you clocked on the documentaries. Far as I could tell they fired about fourteen thousand bullets in a minute.

Which meant you got to be dodging very fast.

There was a crash at the door.

Before they got one step further I was over the desk and I was dragging Louise Bedworth by the hair and by the T-shirt right through the back of their office. Me first so I got a shield if necessary, I learned that.

She screamed and she screamed. She let a load of abuse at me like we were back in the fourth year.

Then hell broke out when their bullets started splattering.

We were on the floor by the door.

'Fucking combination Louise. Fucking combination,' I went.

'1-2-3-4-5.' Never a big brain area the job shop. Got to have one the staff could remember.

I pushed it and we were through. All kinds of noises going down behind us.

'Jesus Nicky!'

'All right Louise?'

'The fuck happening!'

'Wanting something Louise. Not here for the crack. Dunno what. Maybe they want the details of our friend. Like his address, pay his mates a visit.' And maybe they wanted more, like things about his family, his business back home.

'Jesus. And me—'

'And you being the one signed him on, know all about him, they maybe want to ask questions.'

'Fuck. We get out of here Nicky.'

We were out the back door and in the car park. We were away. Down the back doubles. Down the High St. Running with all my shopping. Leave that behind and I get murders off Mum. No bleeding excuses about some shootout.

We stopped way down the market.

'Jesus Nicky.'

'All right Louise?'

'Reckon you . . .'

'Yeah?'

'Reckon you . . . saved my life there Nicky.'

'Nah hardly. They want you alive so you give them the news.'

'Maybe . . . Oh Nicky . . .'

'Nah girl, no need to take on now.'

'Oh Nicky, thank you, thank you. If there's anything I can do for you . . .'

I thought about it.

'Well, now you come to mention it Louise . . .'

'Yeah?'

'You reckon that nervous debility? Like that post traumatic stress disorder?'

'Yeah . . .'

'Might be able to give me an assist on that one Louise.'

'Nicky you are such a bad boy.' She leaned against me and I felt her big tits pressed against me. Tell the truth I was never so interested in that now with Louise, all the more when my ticker was going a thousand to the minute on account of Lithuanians. Still I was hardly going to turn down a feel.

More to the point, I got Noreen stitched. Unfit for work, never have to sign unemployed again. I got a straight up witness for my trauma so now I only needed a tame quack for my Sickness. It was looking good for benefits six months at least without even trying.

ELEVEN

Finally I made my visit to Jimmy Foley up Whipps Cross still carrying Mum's shopping. He was out of Intensive now.

He was surrounded by birds.

Geezers in the bargain. Dean Longmore and Mercedes Marty Fisherman who lifted a motor for taking a few of the birds up. Lift another for taking them home again. Wayne Sapsford in some green strides and a green jacket, fell off a load of turf maybe. Wayne reckoned he was a vestment retailer this week. Elvis Littlejohn looking sharp. But it was the birds for Jimmy.

He was still drowsy. Kind of semi-conscious. Bit like

normal in fact. Three visitors at a time they kept telling everyone only no-one took notice. Elvis smiled at the nurses and they went wobbly.

'All right Jimmy?' I goes.

'All right Nicky?' He raised his mitt kind of feeble.

'You all right now Jimmy, am I right? Got them birds dribbling, yeah?'

'Nicky you heard about my exit wounds?'

'I heard Jimmy mate I heard.' Jimmy loved exit wounds. He got exit wounds, he got birds. 'I heard you got all your problems solved, am I right Jimmy?'

'Nicky they just loving me, you hear what I'm saying?'

'You do anything about it yet Jimmy?'

'Not hardly yet Nicky. Bit low on the old energy levels you understand me. Kind of a bad case of brewer's, know what I mean?' His eyelids were closing and he was yacking slower and slower. 'Only it never be long Nicky I'm hoping, do some little bird a favour maybe evening visiting tonight, yeah?'

'Yeah Jimmy. Go for it mate.' Chantel Livingstone sitting beside me and stroking his paw. He got an exit wound in his paw. All in all he got several exit wounds so she start there and get to the business areas later on.

'Nicky I owes you good, you hear me? I heard you saved me from them gangsters, threw me round so half their bullets went flying over the top, yeah?'

'Jimmy, you and me is like that innit?'

'Yeah.'

'Mates is mates. Don't even think about it son. What you do you do. No problem.'

'Jesus Nicky. I owes you good.'

'Don't owe me nothing Jimmy. Pass on one of them birds when you get tired of her is all.'

'Reckon I will Nicky. Reckon I will.' Then he was out cold and snoring. They thought maybe we zapped him so they fucked us all off out. We went up the canteen for a spliff. We heard now you could get it on prescription for MS so we did wonder about putting Mercedes Marty in a wheelchair for an emergency but we negatived it. Anyhow get Marty in anything with wheels and he steal it, last seen doing ninety down Whipps Cross Rd. So we had a roll up in the canteen and then we went off. I went up Mum's with the shopping and for meeting TT.

Mum never offered me the dosh for all the shopping I got her. True to form.

She passed the rosie round.

There was TT and O'Malley and a fresh inspector from Chingford and a geezer with a hat, got to be from the Yard. There was Mum and Sharon and Kelly and Sharon's kid and Kelly's and my kid Danny. Shithead was at work where he belonged.

Mum even got the ginger biscuits out seeing as the Yard was there.

'Thank you Mrs Burkett. A nice cup of tea.'

'I ain't Mrs Burkett but don't let that trouble you.'

'We need to talk to your son.'

'Big boy he can turn round and talk for himself.'

'We were wondering, er, about privacy. The children and that. And these two young ladies.'

'That's my Sharon and that's Kelly who Nicky got Danny with.'

'Yes . . .'

'We go in my old room,' I went. Privacy never arrived round Priory Court. 'Mum kept it like a shrine so I hear, never touch it in case I want to come back.' We went in. An old suite was tipped all over it when they got the new one, and some dirty mugs and plates where someone came in to watch the other TV. Me I always kept my gaff immaculate since I spent my time in a cell. Maybe a dose of porridge do Mum good as well.

We sat around where we could.

'Nicky,' went the Yard man familiar.

'John,' I went. Never knew his name.

'You saw what happened in the Job Centre.'

'Correct.'

'It has been decided up high that you should not be exposed further to this kind of danger.'

'Bit late innit?'

'Well, maybe. And perhaps reasonable decisions to the contrary were made earlier but now we have decided that they were unreasonable.' He was losing me here. 'It is becoming clear that these villains are serious people.'

'Very large.'

'We don't think you should be asked to go any further in helping police with their enquiries.'

I could see where this was headed.

'I already did,' I went.

'What?'

'Got his address where you kept him. Flat 1, 4 Bolt St, Stratford. Planning a visit, see what goes down, if they're watching.'

'How did you get it?'

'And offer my condolences course.'

'There is no-one there.'

'And them villains know that? And know the address?'

'They may do both by now.'

'But I show myself like I did the bargain with the DI. Question of respect innit? Did the bargain, say no more.'

'He's still unconscious.'

'Poor feller. Line of duty. Least I can do as member of the public and that. Help apprehend the villains.'

'Nicky, you got to give the money back,' goes TT. Ahead of the game. Yard man was supposed to give me a way out, then I felt obliged to make a handback.

'Money don't come into it. I got my bargain with my man. Geezer's word is his bond. Believe that very strong. Never let the DI down.'

'You got to give the money back. The Yard came in.'

'Like I was saying, I carry out my promise so then natural I get to keep the dosh, only fair. And anyhow seeing as I already spent it, went out, couple of shandies and a take-away and then I got to pay my commissions.'

'In addition you are becoming our major witness. Soon they must become aware of this. There is a chance that you will be in serious danger.'

'More reason for keeping the dosh, yeah? Make a getaway?' I knew the bit about the danger. I was already shitless in spades. I wanted to get somewhere out the borough. Canvey Island or Barbados.

'We are putting men on you now Nicky. For your safety. We want to reassure you that they will be there day and night.'

'Day and night? Fuck, you watch everything? Indoors?'

'We watch the building.'

Yeah and some. Watch the building maybe. Then get the machinery out and listen to every squeak indoors. And so far they were never very successful preventing anyone doing a bit of shafting, the way it looked from my area.

'It shouldn't be for long. We intend to move in on them in a couple of days. Bag them.'

'Oh yeah?' I reckoned if they knew so much they got them already. They knew about as much as I knew. Fuck all.

TWELVE

'NOREEN LEAVE IT out,' I went.

'What Nicky?'

'You know for sure they got us wired. Earhole every word. And every little squeak. And you know how you make them little squeaks.'

She giggled. 'And not you Nicky I suppose? You never make them squeaks? On account of it's more like a shouting when you get started, am I right?'

'Noreen . . .'

'Never do them Old Bill any harm to hear a bit of proper good loving, know what I mean?'

'Noreen!'

We were in bed watching the TV and same as usual when we took the TV in the bedroom she started with a little cuddle and then sure as night followed day she started touching me up. Something about the TV got to be, maybe it was electro-erotic waves how I read about somewhere. Give you brain tumours. Me I was quite happy watching the TV in the front room where it belonged, only every now and again like once a week Noreen wanted it in the bedroom. Not usual on a Friday night only this was never a usual Friday.

'Nicky we got to talk.'

'That what you call it Noreen. Talking what you do with the verbals not the fingers?'

'Look no hands. We got to chat now.'

'However you want Noreen, only remember about the wiring, you got what I'm saying?'

'We get under the covers.'

'Noreen you don't reckon they got the bed bugged? You heard about them bed bugs?'

'Nicky they ain't electronic them bed bugs. Thems is them little creepy crawly bed bugs. And no I don't reckon they got the bed bugged. Come on down.'

We got under the duvet. There was a nature programme on TV. I didn't watch out there'd be another one under the duvet.

'Nicky what you reckon we do about Elena?'

'Who?'

'And about getting you out the area?'

'Elena Noreen?'

'Elena who her man told you about.'

It came back slowly.

'The geezer . . .'

'Only the geezer who died Nicky. And the geezer who gave you the necklace and the passport.'

'Oh him.'

'Who got his wife and children waiting for him back in lonely Lithuania.'

'Children Noreen? He mentioned anything about them kids? Had a word in your ear maybe while I was out getting a pint of lager?'

'More than likely got little Jonas aged five. Curly haired and blue eyes and got a big wide loving smile . . . Then little Elena three years old. Laughing back home waiting for her daddy . . . And little Ivan only six months . . .' She started leaking.

'Noreen no-one ever turned round and said a dickie about no kids, no bleeding little Ivan!'

'Bound to be . . .'

'And you remember how he's a fucking gangster Noreen. Gangsters don't get kids. Here, you see what that gorilla just did to that other gorilla? Give me ideas.'

'Come back down Nicky. Concentrate. Watch the TV later.'

'You reckon you can get in that position Noreen? Up a tree?'

She smacked me.

'Nicky I reckon you got to get out the area straight off. And stay out a week or two at least.'

'I was thinking of going down Mum's Noreen—'

'And not just down Priory Court Nicky—'

'Or Clacton or somewhere up some caravan.'

'Too dangerous round here. Got to get well away.'

'What I was thinking.' This was turning out too good to be true. Most birds no matter how sexy and loving they were and that, some time you needed a breather. Few days down the seaside. Or round with your mates. Trouble was that was never how they saw it. Birds, how they came down was they wanted to be together with you all the time. Excepting when they wanted a night out with their mates. You reckoned you wanted to be away, they reckoned it meant you never loved them no more, which was not always the case. So when they reckoned you needed a bit of daylight, well, you got it laughing.

Best not to be too eager though.

'Except I never wanting to be away from you course Noreen innit? You coming with me or what?'

'Oh Nicky. But I got my work.'

'And you got your work, natural. Never take you away from your career structure.'

'Sometimes you can be right considerate Nicky.'

'Mention it Noreen. Ain't nothing.'
'So Nicky I was thinking see . . .'
'Yeah?'
'About you going out to Lithuania tomorrow . . .'

You got to wonder about Noreen. How it was, when she wanted me not committing my crimes and not stabbing geezers and not going anywhere good and not being any geezer except whoever she wanted me to be, how it was she was sending me off on foreign countries and getting into nasties. I reckoned maybe she got some sort of problem in her personality. More particular, maybe she got that problem where you wanted to do something only you never do it so you wanted some other geezer doing it. Prison psychologists told me about that one when they were recommending I never be let back on the street. Fortunate no-one in prison gave a monkey's fuck what the psychologists said or I be there still. Only I never could remember if it was me wanting to do something how some other geezer did it or the other geezer wanting to do it how I did. Psychologists reckoned my mum was in there somewhere in the bargain. And probably her mum.

I lay there clocking the gorillas on the TV. They never got these problems how I saw it. What they were doing, there was no doubting they were doing it and they knew they were doing it and they fucking wanted to be doing it and they never wanted no other gorilla doing it for certain.

'Noreen you run that by me again?' I went. 'I was wondering maybe I got a major infection blockage of the inner earhole.'

'Nicky I was saying I think it best you go out to Lithuania tomorrow.'

'Noreen?'

'Yes Nicky?'

'You turned round and said Lithuania?'

'Yes Nicky.'

'Tomorrow?'

'Yes Nicky.'

'You don't want no sooner than that?'

'Tomorrow be about right Nicky.'

'How you reckon we arrange that then? Tomorrow?'

'I already done it Nicky. Hope you don't mind.'

'You what?'

'On the Internet. When you were in the bathroom.'

'What?'

'Got to be on the Internet. Bleeding useless any other way.'

'Internet Noreen?'

'On the computer Nicky.'

'We got a computer?'

'I borrowed a laptop from work Nicky. Just in case.'

'For buying a ticket?'

'Like I was saying, bleeding useless any other way. Never even get started.'

'You tried down the Central?'

'Nicky they give you a ticket up Oxford Circus. Maybe even Southend. Not Vilnius.'

I got to try and remember that word Vilnius. Kind of name kept escaping me. Like some cousin lived in Sligo.

'I tried the British International. No bleeding use at all. British can't sell you any kind of ticket further than Berlin, would you believe.'

'Never believe it Noreen.'

'They stopped when they got privatised. So I tried all the countries on the way.'

'Noreen you did all this when I was in the bathroom?'

'Mens always did take longer than womens in the bathroom Nicky. And in everything else. Excepting in one thing.'

'Not always the case with you Noreen. On all them things. Specially that last thing. Known you be as quick like a rat out of a trap.'

'Shut it Nicky. So I tried the German website. Got all the information I wanted. So I booked them tickets and you go tomorrow morning. Waterloo. I come down and see you off being as it's Saturday.'

I lay there still staring at the TV and wondering I needed a life check. According to how I was hearing the vibes, here I was laying in my gaff on Howard Rd in the middle of Friday night. Over the weekend I got to get out of the borough to miss a bunch of Lithuanian bazookies who might be giving me serious grief, and then again a small shitload of leery CID trying to snoop me round Walthamstow and get their dosh back. My plan was on avoiding both parties only still going down the football on account of West Ham were at home, then getting a few pints down and investigating a few parts of Noreen where other geezers never reached. All seemed like a fair plan. Maybe take her down South London for the weekend.

Instead she was after telling me in a few minutes I was off catching a fucking train for fucking Lithuania.

'Noreen?' I went weak.

'Yes Nicky?'

'It far on their train?'

'Quite far Nicky I'm hearing. About two and a half days.'

I never asked her to repeat herself. Next time might be worse.

'They got planes go to Lithuania?' I asked gentle.

'Ain't you been hearing how no-one going by plane no more Nicky? Far too dangerous mate. And then again how all them planes spoil the world, all that pollution?' This was Noreen, smartest looking bird in the BA office up west, doing her sales talk. 'No Nicky. I reckon, keep you safe, you go on the train you hear me?'

Keep me safe I wouldn't be going at all.

'Noreen?' I went feeble.

'Yes Nicky my lover?'

'One bit you still got to run by me again, maybe I missed a little bit?'

'Yes Nicky?'

'Why it is I going there? Except getting out the area, I heard on that bit. Only why Lithuania? Not Canvey Island?'

'You got to see Elena. And her little children. You got to tell her about Jonas. And the little children. Then you got to give her that necklace. Then you got to give her that passport. Then you got to find out why he gave them to you, why it all was so important like.'

'You don't reckon it was so important just on account of he was croaking? Loved his bird and that?'

'Nicky let me tell you there was more than that. Mens is not so romantic.'

'No?'

'He was telling you something. Only her name and address, maybe that's romantic. That package though, that was important. It telling you. Either that necklace or that passport, you with me?'

'With you Noreen.'

'Good.'

I waited one moment.

'Only one more question now,' I went.

'One more question Nicky.'

'Who gives a fuck?'

'Pardon?'

'Who gives a flying toss what that package means?'

She put on the patient viz. She even stroked my paw. She snuggled up beside me. 'Now Nicky you got to get a good bit of rest,' she went.

'Excuse me?'

'You got to be a knight in flying armour soon. Take a sad story and tell it like it is. Let them see your female bits.'

Female bits? The fuck she on about?

She gave me a little kiss on the chops, kind of affectionate, kind of I was her big strong thick geezer always stand by her and do something stupid.

The gorillas finished on TV. They seemed happy. They were guzzling away on the old leaves and they seemed like they got any problems in the personal relations area sorted.

One similarity though you got to notice.

The geezer gorilla, he did everything the bird gorilla told him. Even when he looked like he was in charge you could tell she got it all sorted. You could reckon she made all the decisions like what they had for their tea and where they took their holidays.

They got trouble in the jungle she more than likely sent him off to Lithuania too.

THIRTEEN

B RUSSELS GOT MORE stations than Walthamstow.
Walthamstow got St James St then the Central then
Wood St. On the tube it got Blackhorse Rd then the
Central. Then it got that line nobody went on, came out of
Leyton then Queen's Rd then Blackhorse Rd then dis-
appeared somewhere up fucking Tottenham. So counting
the Central and Blackhorse Rd twice Walthamstow got
seven stations. Enough stations for anyone you might be
thinking.

Brussels though, it got more.

It got Brussels Midi where we came in. They put it like
Walthamstow Central, by the precinct handy for the

shoppers. Then they got a Central in the bargain. Hard to credit they wanted a Midi and a Central, bound to cause confusion for the punters. Then they got a north station and a south station. Then I lost count. They got so many it was hard to know what they be doing with all their stations.

On all of them it was raining. Except Central which was like in the tombs underground. It was never cheery catching a train in Brussels.

Noreen she put me on the chuffer up Waterloo.

'Now you be a good boy Nicky,' she went patting my mitt.

'Noreen you sure this train goes up Albania?'

'Lithuania Nicky. Now we been through this already. You take the Eurostar up Brussels. Then you get off. You look for their train up Cologne, what they call Köln. You catch it.'

'Just like that Noreen? Like changing up Finsbury Park?'

'Then up Cologne Nicky you wait two hours then you catch their train goes to Minsk . . .'

'Noreen you making me kind of weary. You want to be changing places or what? You go seeing this Elena and all her kids, being as you know why I'm going, take their package, leave me here on my tod minding my business?'

'And we went through all that Nicky, how me having a job and that and you not doing nothing—'

'Cooking your meals Noreen. Cleaning that toilet. How my work never done.'

'And we decided that you was best suited for some things. Like that housework. Seems to me like it's same difference going to Lithuania and places, you hear what I'm saying?'

'Noreen you thought about me leaving you all alone and going off foreign? I been foreign before. I been on a train. You name it I done it. Now I'm only wanting for staying up Walthamstow, know what I mean? And what I want to know is, what happens to the dusting when I'm gone, right?'

I tried it all.

'Nicky you do as you're told, yeah?'

Noreen spoked.

'You got all them tickets Nicky?' she carried on.

'I got about a hundred tickets here Noreen. Never understand any of them only I got them.'

'They all there Nicky. You just keep them in order like I sorted them out for you. Except you remember they can't sell you that ticket from Minsk to Vilnius,' she went.

'Minsk?' I turned round and went. I was kind of vague about Minsk.

'You got to buy your own ticket out there for that bit.'

'Minsk?' I went again. Where they made coats probably.

'You just turn round and say "Vilnius please" all polite like.'

'Vilnius?' I was still getting trouble in remembering Vilnius. It was never an easy name to remember like Tottenham or Arsenal.

'And they reckon if no-one speaks English they bound to understand German.'

'Very helpful Noreen. Fussball. Goal. Fuhrer. All the German I knows. You reckon that get me that train ticket?'

'No problem Nicky.'

No problem for her anyway, she was staying up Walthamstow. Go down the market every day and get baked beans and plantain and spuds for your tea.

'Noreen you sure they never got aeroplanes out that way?'

'Nicky we explained all that. And in the bargain you got a phobia.'

'Who me?' I got a phobia? First I ever heard.

'No Nicky I want you back here all safe and sound and in one piece, no crashes no phobias. Now you catch this train, yeah?'

Fair enough.

'How long you turned round and said it takes Noreen?'

'Two and a half days out Nicky.'

'Be grey and got a pod by the time I get back. False railings and got a beard.'

'Only twenty-four hours back though Nicky. Kind of speedy.'

She was never putting me on neither. It was straight up.

FOURTEEN

S O SATURDAY MORNING we had one last quick one on account of she already did my packing the night before and we woke up early and got to pass the time somehow. In fact we had one last quick two. We did it before breakfast only then she reckoned I never remember that one seeing as I was half asleep so we got to do it again. I remembered this one anyhow. Not only I was total cream crackered by now. In the bargain she scratched half my shoulder off so I got to put antiseptic on three days. Looked like I got in an argument with a polar bear.

Then she made me another breakfast on account of it being Saturday, her turn, and anyhow I needed it by now.

I got three boiled eggs, kind of a speciality of Noreen's. In my bag she put six bananas. Turned out I had to eat them at Waterloo, already gone brown from being in the bag. Three apples, two oranges, four Mars Bars and thirteen jam sandwiches.

Not all the same kind of jam though. She fancied variety. There was Kwiksave strawberry jam and then again there was Sainsbury's strawberry jam. Then there was a flask of tea. Good job I was never flying or I got to pay out a large one for excess.

She waved me off at Waterloo like I was gone for good. Maybe I was.

I never went to Brussels before but Eurostar was the same as it went to Paris except it went to Brussels. All the couples went off to the toilet soon as it started to join the mile high club. As it goes all the geezers were only wanting a sit down with a lager and the football pages being as it was Saturday, but all their birds were dragging them off to the toilets for an up and under. Came back looking pleased with themselves anyhow, make a good start with their weekend in Brussels.

And all round there were single birds. English and French and Belgian. All on their tod. Ready for it. Probably panting. I never got any offers.

Mobiles going off and going on. It was just the same as in England. 'Je suis dans le train.' Be a bit of a surprise if they turned round and said they were running behind the fucking train. Or lying underneath.

I snoozed looking forward to my few days bird-free. Get a bit of a rest. I got some music and Noreen popped in the Oxfam shop the day before and got me half a dozen books for the trip. None of them about football, most of them written by women before a war or two.

Woke up and found we were in Brussels. No problem.

I heard about their chips off someone I met up the market who reckoned he went to Belgium once and their chips were better than a curry and a lager and a pocketful of Es. While he was telling me he dribbled. I wondered they were as good as he made out. So I got out some English dosh and I found a chippie on the station and they were happy enough taking plenty of my money. The geezer spoke Froggie as well as Belgian so I was all right there, learned Froggie kind of fluent off Marigold our fucking brilliant French teacher after she took us up France, so he asked me how I was getting on round their country and I told him as far as I could see it was all right up Belgium. Then I found out not only they spoke French they did these fucking amazing chips just like the geezer off the market turned round and said. Only problem they put salad cream on them, maybe they were all colour blind and reckoned it was ketchup, still I never wanted to argue. They were worth coming to Belgium for. Back home unless you got chips in some bird's gaff, and some bird who could cook, you got to go up the Chinese for chips. Chinese were the only takeouts knew how to make proper chips. Answer lay in keeping the oil fresh. Keep using old oil and all you got was sog. Round Belgium though it seemed they knew about the oil and were never mean. Their chips were hot and crisp and snappy. Just for making sure it was never a fluke I got another lot off another chippie just outside the station. Same again. Beautiful.

So when my belly was full I went off to Germany. Köln it turned round and said. Noreen even reserved me a seat so I got on their train and I sat in my seat. Not too sure what came after Germany, worry about that when the time came.

We got to Cologne just when the football turned out.

Borussia Dortmund supporters all over the station. Geezers in hats, scarves, jackets, boots, yelling. Or singing, hard to tell the difference. Geezers everywhere. It was like West Ham playing fucking Leeds year ago. Kind of violent leery. Made me real nostalgic, wanted to join in and give out a good slapping. Instead I had to stand around and watch.

I got a pizza in Cologne and looked round for the next train. According to Noreen it was the 7.28 for Minsk. I wandered about.

I clocked it.

Jesus.

It was going on to Moscow. Fall asleep the wrong time and you finished up in Russia.

All they marked on the boards was Warsaw and

Moscow. They spelled them different but it was the 7.28 and it was heading out that way. And Noreen put some dosh in my mitt she reckoned was Polish before I started off, along with the jam sandwiches, reckoned I might be needing it which seemed like some clue. I knew where Warsaw was. I knew Moscow was the other side. I got to hope Minsk was somewhere on the way like and they remembered to stop there.

Still who gave a fuck. See what turned out.

All along the train geezers in uniform were standing outside their coaches. I was looking for coach 153. I walked all the way down and there it was at the end, half way to Minsk already. And would you believe it we got a bird working on our coach.

Big strong woman in the bargain. Legs like a lumberjack. Arms as big as my legs. Blonde. Bust like a bulldozer. Waist went in and out again. Like Death Valley. She put her mitts on her hips and clocked me like I was a speck of dust on the end of her hooter.

I gave her my best friendly one. White teeth. Mince pies twinkling.

'All right Lara?' I goes.

She went something in Russian. Sounded like she just spat me out.

'You the boss woman then mate or what? See you and me are going to be best friends. Go for a pint later, know what I mean?'

She grabbed my tickets out my mitt. Clocked them. Saw London on them. Cackled. Geezers being from England gave her a good laugh. She went something else in Russian then she beckoned me in her carriage.

I never could resist birds in uniform. She got a short skirt and you could sniff every bit of her rippling. When she walked up the steps to her carriage she got one cheek going one way, one cheek going the other. I wanted her thighs keeping me locked securely in my place.

She pointed me in a cubbyhole about a quarter the size of a prison cell. She reckoned that was my bedroom.

Except there were three places marked. Me and two more. Where you never got room to swing an ant. I never had conditions like this when I was in the nick. Maybe Wandsworth got something going for it after all.

I got in there and I put my bag down and I pulled out my snacks and I made myself comfortable and I started on reading some book by some old bird.

Then after about half an hour when things were just nicely nicely she came in and she stood over me. My boat race was level with her business area.

'All right Lara?' I went calm and collected. She got a badge on reckoned her name was Katya.

'Tea or coffee?' she turned round and said. Except it was in Russian but tea was chai, same as in Pakistan. Coffee was coffee, kind of handy.

'Chai please,' I went seductive.

So she toddled off and she came back with a cup of tea in a glass. In a silver holder with a handle. All free. Jesus I reckoned she liked me, I was in here. Her little beadies were twinkling and she was waving all over. Could be a knee trembler before we even got out of Germany.

Then we stopped. Dusseldorf. She stopped in the bargain, went off and did her bits and bobs somewhere.

Then it stopped again. Duisberg. I knew about all these on account of they got football teams. Then it stopped again. Essen. Lara went past very slowly before we got there and my knees started quivering all on their own.

Except it all went wrong in Essen. Two more geezers came in my cubbyhole.

Shit.

They came in and they stood round speaking some language and looking crowded. Hardly room to stand up. Then she came in and she got a little tool out. She started taking down beds. They came from nowhere out the walls. Yeah they got three. In a pile, one on top the other. She pointed out where we all went.

And guess which one Muggins got.

Stretched out under their ceiling, if I sneezed I hit the roof. Then it was shorter up there in the bargain so I could put my neck straight out or my feet straight out only not both the same time.

Noreen got a lot to answer for.

New geezers were cheery enough. Big strong hard

looking geezers. Spoke their language not English or French or German or Australian. They yacked away to me about something or other, maybe birds or stabbings or football. I passed the time of day in Urdu which I picked up a smattering of, only they never seemed fluent in Urdu. Their language sounded like someone sneezing. Good job they never took the top bunk or they hit the ceiling every time they spoke.

They were off home by the look of it. They got cases full of clothes and that so I guessed they were working somewhere, going east for a spot of home leave. They got bags of sandwiches and Mars Bars and then they took the vodka out. Passed them all round, made the evening go sweeter. Cheery geezers. Not their fault they just spiked my international relations.

'Prost,' they went.

'And you too geezers,' I went. 'Just about to ask for a touch of the other when you came along, dunno my chances but worth popping the question I reckon, still don't let it bother you fellers. Always some other bird, you hear what I'm saying?'

'Arrivederci,' they went, reckoned it meant the same.

'No problem geezers.'

After a couple of hours I curled in a ball in my top drawer and went to kip. Woke up a couple of hours later. Went to kip again. Woke up an hour later. Went to kip again. Woke up twenty minutes later. It was like sleeping with a new woman. I was just dozing off nicely again when we got visitors.

Four o'clock in the morning three Old Bill banging on your door, you know you got serious grief. Except in Walthamstow they did it at six o'clock, too lazy for getting up earlier our Old Bill.

They were banging on our door and opening it whatever we did. Three big pigs in thick coats.

'All right fellers?' I went. Always be civil to the fuckers that time of the morning. Never let them clock you upset, make it look like you were always expecting them and just about to put the kettle one.

'Passport,' they went.

We were crossing some border. Whatever country came next, we were going in it.

'Passport,' they went again.

Then I clocked they never spoke English so it was no matter what I turned round and said to them.

'Jesus,' I goes, 'you fuckers don't know when's the time for waking a geezer, am I right? You fuckers ain't got no women and children to go home to or what you fucking slimeballs?'

'Passport,' they went.

I found it under my pillow. Gave it to them. They stared at it. Turned it round. Had a little yack about it among themselves. Started cackling. Had another butcher's. Decided they might as well stamp it. Gave it back.

'English,' they went. Then they fucked off.

Next morning all the land was flat as a chapatti. All the stations started with a Z. Far as I could guess it we got to be in Poland.

It was snowing in Warsaw. Warsaw got even more stations than Brussels and it was snowing on all of them. It was snowing all the way to Belarus.

Back in England it wasn't snowing. Back in England it was warmer. You might turn round and say England was better.

How I knew I was going to Belarus was when Noreen informed me she went down their embassy at lunchtime to get me a visa. I reckoned a visa was something you nicked out of a handbag.

'Belarus?' I went weak.

'Belarus yeah.'

'That a place or a country?'

Turned out it was one or the other. It was one of the most miserablist experiences of my life. Fact in truth they only got one thing really going for them Belarussians. They got the last country on earth where you still got a real live pukka bag of peanuts.

Fortunate as it goes Noreen packed all my jam sandwiches. Twenty-four hours there was nothing solid on the chuffer you could buy. My geezers in my compartment and everyone else they all took jam sandwiches. We got over another border from Poland to Belarus, more fucking Old Bill in big coats, then we stopped three and a half hours in Brest. No special reason it seemed like, maybe they liked the name. While we were waiting there in some siding some old biddy came up retailing a packet of old doughnuts by the widow. She was just a bit happy for taking some Polish note I gave her so it was likely ten times the price. I was happy, ate six doughnuts. Then we stared at the ceiling till the train got itchy again and we carried on. We were in Belarus.

Thing about the peanuts is, back in England they got this problem with the packets. In the old days they made bags of peanuts so you pulled them apart at the top and there you were, Bob's your fucking uncle. Then some fucking smart-arse probably did some course decided you got to tear them down some fucking line just so no-one could get them coming out easy and normal, only one or two at a time and then when they did come out the fucking peanuts went everywhere. No fucking consideration for the punter at all. Specially when you got a few pints inside you, peanuts were all over the fucking boozer and out the door. Probably some marketing plot so you fucking spilled them and got to buy another fucking packet. In Belarus they made them so you pulled the packet apart all nice and fucking dandy and you put all your little fingers in and take out one peanut or five peanuts or all the fucking peanuts at once, just however you went and fucking chose it. Personal choice type of thing.

So Belarus rated quite high on the clapometer already, far as I was concerned.

I got my peanuts in some swanky hotel Noreen booked me in.

It was only when I got to Minsk I realised just how many problems I got. First off I couldn't even read Minsk on the station. It said something else altogether. In funny letters.

All the passengers were telling me it was Minsk though so I took their word for it. I got my bag and said my see yous to my geezer mates then I got off their train.

It was cold as a witch's tit.

I went out the station. Noreen told me get a cab from the station to the hotel. Only problem was I couldn't remember the name of the hotel and I couldn't read it neither in their letters. I went out the station and I clocked a cab on the street. I went up the cabbie and I gave him an East End smile. Heart of gold type.

'All right mate?' I went

'Sputnik,' he went. Or something resembling.

'Dollars mate?' I went. Somewhere on the way I picked up some US dollars. Never remembered how and never knew what the fuck they were worth anyhow.

'Dollars,' he went smug. Turned off his meter straight off for dollars. Got all his wits about him, no messing with the regulations.

I showed him the hotel name.

'Sputnik,' he went again. Then we were off.

Occurred to me on the way maybe I was being hijacked by the Mafia in a yellow cab. Maybe reckoned I was a rich geezer and my mum was likely for paying a star's ransom to get her boy back. Never knew my mum. Then I reckoned I never looked like a rich geezer round there. Everyone I clocked so far in Minsk looked a whole lot richer. All got big coats for a start off. Woolly hats and boots. Specially Old Bill. So I thought relax, either your time has come or it never.

He took me straight up my swanky hotel. All the time he lifted the dollars out of my mitt he was trying hard to stop cackling while he counted. Never seemed a lot to me, he probably reckoned he was shafting me but he never got shafted by a London cabbie. Made him look like a fairy. So he put me down and I gave him thanks and he gave me the thumbs up so he was happy anyhow and I went in the door of their hotel.

It was bigger than Hackney stadium.

It went round in a curve and up into their sky. Its hall was bigger than a football pitch, play a game in there and still got room for a basketball court. And the toilets. In the distance was their desk so I went on a sponsored walk across there and met a very strict woman.

'All right missis?' I went. 'Nicky Burkett here. Very pleased to make your acquaintance and that. I reckon you got me a bedroom.'

'Mr Burkett,' she went. Accurate so far but hard to tell if she spoke English from that.

'Bit of a pleasure zone you got here then?' I went. 'See you got a night bar in the distance there. Spot of clubbing later?'

She handed me a key. 'Go to your room,' she turned round and said. She spoke English.

So I went. My room got a TV with nine channels. Would you believe every one of them was Russian.

My bed though was different from last night's and quite a long way off the ceiling. I reckoned on some catching up only first I reckoned on getting something in my stomach. It was ten o'clock and I went for the night bar.

Which was where I got the peanuts.

They got plenty of beer but all they got in the food line was one cheese sandwich. Least it was half a cheese sandwich on account of they only made one side of bread. Then they got ten packets of peanuts. So I had all that.

In the bar with my beer and half a sandwich and ten bags of peanuts I wondered just what the fuck I was doing there.

Then I went to my pit.

FIFTEEN

I SLEPT TEN HOURS straight off then I came down and got breakfast of four hard boiled eggs and cereal and eight pieces of black bread and jam and a spot of cabbage. Came off a buffet kind of a pick and mix so there was no argument.

Couple of old Americans came and sat with me. Spoke English. After a fashion. Super smiley. They reckoned they got a lot of friends in Minsk. Soon as they reckoned they got a lot of friends somewhere like Minsk you knew they got to be telling porkies. Sure enough they were God botherers. Visiting a whole lot of other God botherers. I made my excuses and went off up for another shower.

Then I went round Minsk. My train didn't go till dark. Minsk was kind of unbelievable.

It got huge fucking great buildings everywhere. Nothing like it in Walthamstow. Even the new complexes up Stratford were like minnows. It never said what any of them were, palaces or parliaments or post offices or museums or secret Old Bill shops but they were the biggest buildings I ever clocked anywhere. Every one of them bigger than Buckingham Palace. Whole city was kind of mega. Then I went for a pizza.

I was having a spot of bother spending all my dosh. The night before I changed a score. Seemed only reasonable. They gave me forty thousand roubles. Seemed like a lot of roubles for twenty quid but I reckoned maybe it was special treatment, bird liked the cut of my jib. Anyhow I went in a supermarket and bought some more peanuts then I got a coffee then I went down the station and bought the ticket for Vilnius Noreen never got. No problem as it goes, just went 'Vilnius please' like Noreen turned round and said and they wrote down some roubles and I gave it over. Then I got a cup of chai. Still it never seemed to make any impression on my forty thousand roubles. Jesus. Bit of a problem. Best I could think of was keep going in the toilet up the station, least that was a hundred and fifty roubles every time. And being as it was so fucking cold out, all I could think of anyhow was going and having a Jimmy.

So I went and got another pizza. Never wanted it much,

still it passed the time and they spoke English in their big pizza place. Maybe they reckoned it was strange a geezer getting two pizzas in a day, still they never said. Then I went for another gander round town and crossed the river and clocked a feller sitting on a chair on the ice. It was so cold by the river my feet turned blue.

They got a lot of blondes in Minsk. All round town half the women were blonde. And I reckoned all the blondes were giving me the glad eye. Other half never seemed fussed some reason. You had to ask an interesting question, was it blondes fancied the look of a geezer from England?

Say what you like about Russian women, I was expecting them short and squat and kind of husky. Instead there were some real lookers, tall and blonde and perky. Bit of a bonus.

I got down the station a couple of hours early for their train, nothing else to do except go to the toilet now and then. I got a few coffees. Then half an hour before it went I started looking for it. Just as well.

I got on the train two minutes before it went. Never find the platform. Asked around everyone, no bleeder understood me. Searched the fucking station. Then eventual I went 'Vilnius Vilnius!' to some geezer on platform one and he waved off in the distance like you had to walk there, and way down the bottom of some platform out in the country I found some boxes on wheels. First off

I reckoned it was for horses, then I jumped inside and two minutes later we were off.

Everyone really cheery. Conductor woman smiled at me. Other passengers smiled at me. Gave me grub. Cups of coffee. I tried for giving away some roubles seeing as I never had more use for them. Everyone cackled, no thank you very much. Old Bill came in at the border wanting to spoil everyone's day only no-one took any notice. All very pleased to be going home it seemed like.

Maybe Lithuania was never going to be so bad after all.

But I reckoned Minsk was cold till I got to Vilnius.

I walked out their station and the inside of my hooter froze up.

First I reckoned I got some sudden large bogey fell out of my brain somewhere. Then it felt like I breathed in a whole bunch of spiders. Then it hit me. Their frost got me. All the way up the nostrils was solid. It was crinkly and it was hard.

The train got to Vilnius about ten o'clock. I never clocked a thing on the way on account of it was dark. According to Noreen the hotel where she booked me was three minutes away across the street and round the corner. So I stepped out the station and my hooter froze up. Then my knees fell off.

Down to the waist I was pukka. On top I was wearing an old balaclava I bought years back when I fancied taking up bank robbing till I saw the queues up the Halifax. Below I got a T-shirt and two shirts and a jumper and a jacket out of the army surplus. So the top half was getting by. On my feet I got three pairs of socks in my boots. Given half a chance they'd be right as rain. Problem was by the time the blood reached the feet it was frozen solid. All I got between them and my top half was pants and jeans. It was so cold down there I looked for making sure I never forgot to put my jeans on at all. I was worried about the future of my short and curlies. Tomorrow it was going to be two pairs of strides no problem.

I never went in a hotel before I met Noreen. I reckoned they were never for geezers from Walthamstow. She reckoned you just booked and you went there and they curtsied and dusted your eyebrows. I tried to slunk in without them noticing, case they spotted straight off where you came from and you got no business there. My mum never stayed in a hotel. Sharon my sis her visiting massage service got called to them occasional, the Alfred Hitchcock or the Sleeping Beauty down by Baker's Arms but that was never the same. I was the first member of the family ever stayed in one and I'd be pleased I never did it again.

I found it just where Noreen turned round and said.

'All right mate?' I went to the geezer behind the desk. 'Laba diena and that?' I got my Lithuanian phrasebook Noreen supplied.

'Good evening, I believe you are from Walthamstow,' he went.

'Priory Court mate as it goes. It stamped on my bonce or what?'

'A lady telephoned. She said she was your missis. I believe that may be like a wife. She said I should tell you to be a good boy.'

'Sounds like Noreen. Kind of a bird more than a wife. You were expecting me anyhow. Pleased to meet you. And you never half speak the lingo good, am I right?'

'Yes we were expecting you. Your missis Noreen sent us a fax and an e-mail and a letter and then she telephoned to confirm the booking. Then she just telephoned again to make sure you were expected. Yes we were expecting you. In fact we couldn't wait.'

'Very nice of you geezer. And matter of fact I'm right chuffed to be here innit?' I could flannel with the best of them. 'Reckon tomorrow I check out the manor and do a spot of sunbathing, know what I mean?'

'I don't think so,' he went.

Then he got me to sign in and we carried on being friendly. He told me where I got breakfast, almost ready for it by now but he reckoned I had to wait till the morning for it. Then he told me my room number and he suggested how I wandered round upstairs till I found it.

I went in my room and I turned on the TV. They got the BBC, some funny kind of BBC I never clocked before where they told you the same thing every twenty minutes. Still they got the football scores from the weekend. West Ham came second. Good job I left the country.

Then I slept another ten hours.

I was in Lithuania, or Lietuva how they called it round there.

Next day I went looking for Elena.

SIXTEEN

BREAKFAST WAS A DOWNER.

Geezer on the desk was still on duty in the morning. Long shifts it looked like. I could give him counselling about getting the dosh off the dole, maybe some false Housing Benefit and a few dodges and he could get right up to the mark. All the same he seemed happy. He pointed me downstairs for my breakfast. I reckoned on a spot of porridge and the old toast and marmalade, nothing fancy. Heat up for the day then out in their snow.

On my way downstairs I read up what my guidebook turned round and said about the breakfast.

'Hotel Mikotel,' it went. 'This brand new hotel is right

near the train station and across the Hales Turgaviete market. Fortunately unlike both of those places the hotel's interior is clean, bright and modern. The rooms, decorated mostly in soothing blues, greens and cream colours, have only showers and those small beds so common in the Baltic. The reception desk staff is absolutely cheerful. Breakfast is included in the price of the room and served in their cosy breakfast nook.'

You got to hand it to them. I never gave a fuck if the rooms were soothing, and the bed took me in it no problem and the TV in the bedroom was more than I got at home except when we took it out of the living room and the whole gaff was warmer than home in the bargain. Only they never spilled a dickie about their porridge for breakfast.

On account of they never got any.

Nor marmalade.

Nor toast.

First off there was water kind of luke-ish out of a flask. You put your teabag under it, fucking Lipton's in the bargain, after about five minutes it started changing colour slightly and after about ten it was nearly the colour of tea.

Old biddy in charge of breakfast gave me the rosie and told me get all my grub down my gob in Lithuanian.

Grub was set out on your plate for you. They got black bread like on the foreign shelves everyone walked past in the supermarket. And white bread like plastic plates. Then

142

with them a tichy portion of strawberry jam made in some country I never heard of. And a few bits of processed cheese like Dairylea.

You got to say Lithuania never made a good start with their breakfast.

I reckoned give them the benefit of the doubt though, maybe breakfast was kind of their weak spot.

Anyhow I gobbed it all down, everything I could find even the black bread. Then I went out looking for Elena.

I went back past their desk on my way.

'I hoped you enjoyed your breakfast Nicky,' went the cheery geezer.

'Champion mate. Bleeding champion. Fit for the trotters derby now I reckon. Start straight off.'

'I am very happy.'

Took me about half an hour getting all my clobber on. Most important was two pairs of strides. Then I marched out on their street. Pylimo they called it.

It was fucking parky.

Uzupio 18–9. Where Elena lived. Never knew what it meant, Uzupio 18–9. Ought to be easy to find though.

First I got to get breakfast. No point setting out for anywhere except you got a decent cup of rosie in your belly.

Never hold it against the Lithuanians. Geezer in the hotel was a right friendly feller. Only they never knew what they were doing with a breakfast.

I got my map out. First I was headed for what they called the Pub. I stood at the door of the hotel and turned left.

Nobody told me Vilnius was beautiful. It was a fucking killer.

They were tarting up all the old buildings. Good clean up and they looked as good as new except they were all about five hundred years old. It was like down by the courts up London where I went for conferences with my brief before my big cases. And a spot of palaces thrown in. Everywhere was ancient. Turn right anyhow off Pylimo and there you were right in it, in their old town. It was fucking brilliant.

Except it was so bleeding freezing I spent all the time half way running, even when I was standing still for clocking the street names I was running on the spot. My eyelashes were turning blue.

I turned right on Traku by the cinema and kept on up Dominikanu past the church and there it was. They gave it a long name but there were special first letters spelled out P.U.B. It was all for English speakers. Bob's your auntie. I was in there.

I sat straight down at a table and ordered me a pot of tea and it tasted like fucking no-one's business, brown and bitter and beautiful. It was the monte. Then I got some cornflakes. And some toast. And the little darling served me spoke English and she got a body like a little oak tree and her little acorns prodded out and she smiled at me like I was all her tomorrows. It was like being back in Walthamstow. Fact it was a lot better.

'All right darlin'?' I went when she brought the rosie.

'Here is your tea. Welcome to Vilnius,' she turned round and said.

'Welcome ain't hardly in it mate. Reckon you just made one lucky geezer so very bleedin' chuffed he don't hardly know which way the sun shines, know what I mean Heidi?'

'Er, not really.'

'You free after you get off then Heidi, spot of nosh and put a few pints down your neck or what?'

'Thank you very much. Have a nice day.' She was off.

They never full threw off their Russian shackles total yet, otherwise she'd be down my throat.

'See you later.' Reckoned I'd come back and give her a spot of British charming, turn her over with sweet talk. I finished off my tea and had another butcher's at my guidebook and maps, then I dressed up in a few more layers again and went out in the Arctic.

Uzupio was in Uzupis. Some kind of suburb. Crazy name Uzupis, still no accounting. It was fifteen minutes to walk across their old city.

Down a wide road to the Town Hall. Down another big wide road, past the pizza gaff, past the market selling the same old toot as Walthamstow market except no breadfruit, then off right down the side streets, all of it ancient. Five minutes down the side roads and you hit the river. It got ice all along the edges. Then a bridge. Over it, up by a café and there it was. Uzupio.

It looked like it was the High St of Uzupis. Which stood to reason. It was the road all other roads went off. Although it was missing the shops.

All Uzupis was being tarted up like the main city. It was even older in bits. First buildings you came to though were already good as new. They were smart. Different when you went further up the street. Here they still looked kosher at the front, only when you clocked their back yards you could spot how they were still crumbling.

Up the street a bit more and you came to a square. Road was up. Gas mains probably or cable TV. Geezers working. How the fuck they worked in that snow was their business. I went all right to the geezers when I went past, laba diena and that and they went laba diena back. Friendly geezers.

I went on up there and then I got to start taking notice for the address. And for other things. Not much chance I reckoned on finding Elena in there even she lived there. Still give it a whirl. So I got to take notice of a lot.

Number 18 got a number on the front wall.

I clocked it. But I walked straight past and up the hill.

Reason being it was getting surveillance.

Other side of the street a Merc was cruising slow. Up

and down. Back and forward. And it got tinted windows.

Shit. A Merc with tints. Old Bill got Mercs round here? Whatever the fuck it was it was never good news.

I went up and in a circle and round. Up that way the buildings mostly weren't renovated and they were poorer. I looked like a stranger. A stranger who never knew what the fuck he was doing. I came back. I wandered down slow on the other side of the road. The motor was just moving off.

Always a chance there were more doing the undercover up one of the houses. Nothing I could do about that. Some time I got to make my move. I waited maybe fifteen minutes. Went up the road again and back again. Stood around looking like a lemon. Then I crossed over and went up to number 18.

The front door got numbers 1–6.

Now I understood what they were about. Uzupio 18–1 was the first address and number 1 was the first flat. Uzupio 18–2 came next. Made sense. So Uzupio 18–9 was there somewhere only not in the front door, and I got to find it.

I went down the alley by the side and took a gander round the back.

There was a yard. I followed the building right round till I came to another doorway. No numbers on it. I went up to it and pushed the door. It was rickety. Swung open with a little creak. Inside was old, dusty and dark and not done up at all. I stepped over and in.

147

I stood there waiting till I was settled. Got used to the light. Had a little look. On the right were letter boxes. 7–16.

Behind the letter boxes was the door to a flat. It got no number on it. It looked maybe no-one opened it for a couple of centuries.

I went upstairs. Trying to look like a confident geezer wanting for making an investment in shoddy old property. Not succeeding. Looking more like a geezer flogging double glazing to an Eskimo.

On the next floor they got two more doors. Still no numbers. I stood there waiting. What I was waiting for was another matter. Eventual I reckoned there was no purchase in standing about helpless so I went over and knocked one of the doors.

Silence.

Tyla. I got time to look it up in my book. Silence.

Then a sort of shuffling noise like an old dog shifting its bum across a yard.

Then a clanking of locks.

Then the old dog opened the door.

I near as cried out in shock. It was some old bird about four hundred years old. Hair falling straight down the side of her bonce. Old hooter sticking out. No solid food this century, not unless she left her molars down the back of the settee. She opened the door and she clocked me good. Except I was never sure her poor old mince pies clocked anything. She was old.

She went something got to be Russian not Lithuanian. Unless it was on account of the teeth situation. It was half way between spitting and swallowing.

'Laba diena,' I went. I got to learn some more words, this was getting boring.

She beckoned me in over her doorstep. Maybe she reckoned I was the home help. Or maybe she reckoned I was Little Red Riding Hood.

'Elena?' I went not going in anywhere.

'???' she went.

'Elena?' I turned round and said. 'You Elena? Basanavicius and that?'

She gave me the stare.

Then she pointed upstairs. She seemed kind of disappointed.

Got to admit I was never disappointed at all. I was hoping old matey up London never sent his necklace to this old bird. Not being mean like only I was hoping he got someone back home in double figures.

I remembered thank you.

'Achoo,' I turned round and said. 'Achoo.' Felt kind of stupid saying it, still it was their business how they made their words up.

She stood there staring. Maybe she took me for a grandson. I went on upstairs. So Elena did live there.

Maybe she was out at work. Maybe she was down the

market. Maybe she was doing some gangstering somewhere. Still no going back now.

I got up the next stairs. It was old and crumbly round
the hall. Plenty cobwebs. Dark corners. There was one
door on this landing. It was new.

Still no doorbell so I went and banged on it. I was ready
for anything.

But I never expected what I got.

SEVENTEEN

S HE NEVER OPENED first off. She took a butcher's through the Jehovah's Witness hole. Then she had a think. Then she opened a crack. Two dark mincers and a little pointy hooter appeared by the frame.

'Elena?' I went.

She went something Lithuanian.

'Speak English?' I goes.

Long pause.

'I speak English. Yes I speak English. Who are you?'

'Nicky Burkett. From London. Walthamstow. I got something for you.'

'What have you got?'

'Something your feller give me.'

Very long pause.

'You have come from Jonas?' she went.

So she never knew what happened yet. Shit. Not a good start-off.

'Yeah. You let me in?'

She did. Opened the door wide. I went in and she shut it behind.

'Come,' she turned round and said.

We went through her hall and in a big wide room with thick curtains and thick chairs and thick carpets. Pictures on the wall. When you came off that staircase you never believe that gaff was sitting there waiting.

Lighting was quiet. So was her music out of some speaker hidden. Violin type of music. We were quiet.

'Please sit down.'

I did. She sat opposite me.

'Please tell me about Jonas. I have not heard. He has sent you? What has happened? He is coming home?'

There was no point bleeding around the fucking bush.

'Jonas is brown bread lady,' I went. 'Sorry and that. There it is.'

'What? He is what?'

'Er, pardon, sorry Elena, what I mean to say is he got stiffed. Whacked like. He croaked. End of story.'

'End of story?'

'Yeah.'

'It is, what, the end of his story you say?'

'Yeah.'

'He is . . . dead?'

'Yeah.'

Long, long silence. Tyla.

She stood up. Her eyes went wider and wider. Then her head went slowly, slowly down. Her hands stayed down her lap when she sat down again. Then she put them up her boat race. Then she put them down again.

'I knew,' she went.

I let her yack.

'I knew.'

Then she went on in Lithuanian. Then she started rambling. Starting to get hysterical. Wailing. Lifted her bonce. Tears came out dribbling all round. 'I knew,' she went again.

'On account of you never heard nothing?'

'I did not hear from him. Always he called me every two days. I did not hear.'

'Sorry and that.'

She got up and she went in the other room. I sat and waited five. Then I got up and went in the kitchen off the hallway. Found the kettle. Found the tea. Lipton's, hardly fucking better than nothing. No milk in the fridge so I reckoned she took it black. I put sugar in and went through, knocked on her bedroom door and went in. She was curled on the bed. I put the tea down.

'Thank you.'

I went back in the front room.

After another ten she came back and she sat.

We both sat. We sat opposite each other. She put her boat race up.

'Tell me please,' she went.

'You sure you want to know Elena?'

'Yes.'

'You sure?'

'I am sure. What happened, I want to know. Everything.'

I never believed it, not when she heard it.

'Look mate . . .' I went. 'Your Jonas . . . He . . . His life it didn't end off exactly smooth like, you get what I'm saying?'

'Please Mr . . .'

'Nicky. Nicky Burkett.'

'Let me tell you something Nicky. I know all about Jonas. I know he was gangster.'

'Ah.'

'Yes.'

'So—'

'So you can tell me.'

'Oh well then, no problem girl eh?' I breathed out, kind of relieved. We knew the knockings then. Always best when they knew the score.

'No problem Nicky.' She smiled kind of dim. Kind of

slightly leaking still.

'Well Elena, Jonas he got himself stuck in the dole queue innit?'

'Stuck? He got stuck in the what? Some kind of machine? In an elevator?'

'Nah . . . Stuck like shafted, know what I mean? He got stabbed up Elena. Straight in the old heart, clean as a fucking whistle, one minute there he was happy as Larry, next minute whoosh, there he is laying down dead. You never clocked anything like it girl I'm telling you, cleanest bit of stabbing I ever witnessed. All he got time left to do was two things.'

'He was stabbed?' She got there a bit late.

'Like I'm telling you, stabbed right in the coronary area. Bosh. Up and under. No problem. End of story.'

'Oh God.'

'Very quick Elena I'm telling you. He never suffered. Real lucky geezer, know what I mean?'

'Oh God.' Waterworks starting up again.

'You want another cup of tea?'

She shook her bonce. Then she got up and walked round the room and stared out the window. Not the front window.

While she was doing all that I took the oppo for a proper spec of her body parts. She was a bit of a looker was Elena, no doubting it. She was tall like a tree. She got legs up to there. She was thin but she got tits. Shapey. She got long dark hair. She got a round face. Even allowing for she was kind of old like thirty-two or thirty-three, still she looked like she could move with the best of them.

She clocked me giving her the once over. She turned and she stood and then she stared at me. I made out I was viewing the artwork on the walls.

'Nicky,' she turned round and said.

'Yeah Elena?'

'Please can we talk later? I would like a little time alone do you understand?'

'Course Elena. No problem. Nearest and dearest get shafted, natural you want a spot of time on your tod. Come back in half an hour or what?'

'Perhaps three or four hours please. Then we will talk. There is much that I must know.'

'Course Elena. Course.'

They were back.

I went out the alley and round the street. Down towards the river was the tinted Merc. I never liked it.

I walked down past it and went in the café by the river for a coffee. From there I could clock the Merc while the Merc was clocking the gaff.

They were likely for staying there doing surveilling. No reason to come after me. Probable they never knew it was Elena I was visiting there. Could be I was seeing the old witch down below. Maybe I was her grandson up from the sticks, brought her a bag of turnips or a packet of marijuana seeds.

Except I was wearing my trainers off Walthamstow market and a coat off the army surplus and jeans out of Stratford. Just a bit visible. As it goes only one of my pairs of jeans was out of Stratford, the other one I got on was out of Oxford St where Jimmy Foley lifted a whole delivery before he retailed them round the borough.

I went in the café and sat down.

'Laba diena mate,' I went to the waiter geezer.

'Laba diena mate,' he goes. Taking the piss or what?

'Kavos mate,' I turned round and said. 'Prasom.'

He went off. I reckoned I was fluent. Then I reckoned otherwise, on account of I never got the words for the next bit when two geezers with shades and big coats and hats came in and sat down the other end of the room. They came out of the Merc.

I ran down my guidebook, see if it got a handy phrase for the situation. 'Gelbekit!' it went. 'Help!' Only I got no-one to turn round and say it to.

They were dressed too smart for Old Bill and they got Italian shades. They were drinking coffee and vodka. They kept their bonces down. They were never talking. They never looked at me neither.

The waiter geezer came over again.

'Gelbekit mate,' I went. 'Prasant!'

'Taip?' he went.

I leaned my judge in their direction. 'Gelbekit,' I went again. 'Gangsters.'

'Ah!' he turned round and said. 'Kavos?'

I reckoned it must be his cover up, pretend he was getting me coffee.

'Taip,' I went.

He went off in the kitchen. I studied my books. They never got gangsters in there. Never reckoned the need maybe. Criminals was nusikaltelis. Forget that one. Too difficult.

Waiter came back. He went over to the gangsters and he gave them two cups of coffee. Each. Spoke to them. They looked over me.

'Achoo,' they went.

'No problem geezers,' I went.

Just how the fuck I ordered them two coffees each was never very clear but they seemed happy about it. I looked up two in the book. Du. I looked up four. Keturi. Was that like gelbekit? Both got a kit or a ket. Got to be something faulty in my accent. Needed more work.

I paid the geezer and I was out of there before they started on their second coffees. I hoped they wouldn't come after me and leave a good coffee.

They had to be family. As in Family. Not to be mixed with and not people you wanted too friendly or too unfriendly. I went over the bridge and back in the little streets of the old city where it was hard for motors to drive.

Boys in the organised crime, they never liked getting out of their motors and on their plates so maybe they wouldn't come after me. As it goes they stayed where they were, never even left the café while I was watching.

I went back up by the town hall. Followed the streets down to the main river, not the little one by Uzupis. It was near as covered in ice. Big chunks floated down the middle, came out of somewhere even colder. You could almost walk on it. By the edge the water in some parts was frozen solid. One place there was a geezer sat with a fishing rod stuck through a hole in the ice. You had to say there were stupid geezers and then there were stupid geezers. This one maybe got his brain parts mixed with the jelly beans out of the pick 'n' mix. I'd sooner be locked in the toilet with a rattlesnake.

I turned right and walked half a mile and crossed over a bridge and walked along a path by the river covered in snow. Massive buildings like stadiums stood away behind. I carried on up another bridge and there over the road they got a department store. I went in. It was warm.

Fuck that was nice.

I went all over the store clocking all kinds of stuff I never looked at before in a shop. Towels, knickers, coffee pots, washing up bowls. I looked at them at home before and I heard they came from shops but I never found the need to go staring at them. Now I went gazing. Noreen be proud of me, turn into a woman before long.

I found the café in there up the top floor and got another coffee. After an hour or so going round the departments I reckoned it best to go before security started taking an interest so I went out in Siberia again. Back across the river to Gedimino.

In the post office you could get another coffee and I sent Mum a postcard. Glad You Ain't Here. I got warm again in there. Found the bookshop after that. Got warm again in there. Just over the road was their other department store. I spent another hour there and got another coffee and got warm again in there. And used the toilet. Every time I went indoors I got cosy enough, then every time I went out I got fucking freezing again. It was like working in a frozen pea factory.

Around Gedimino and the river they put all their palaces and churches and whatnot. Come back in the summer maybe.

Far as I could tell nobody was following me round Vilnius. I hoped Elena was still in one piece when I got back. I hoped she stayed clear of the men in the Merc and I reckoned she ought to be over her bereavement by now.

EIGHTEEN

I WENT BACK up Uzupis.

I did a very big circuit by the main road and came in from the other side by the graveyard. Hoped we wouldn't be needing their graveyard.

Coming down the hill I checked for tinted motors. None. Checked out doorways. Course they might have her bugged and got geezers on the road gang and pay off the neighbours. Still, they did all that then they got no need for the Merc in the first place, so it seemed like the street was clean.

Went down the other side of the road to the bottom, then back up where I started, then back down her side and slip in her alleyway.

JEREMY CAMERON

In the main door and up the stairs.

This time I gave the old biddy a miss. Straight on up to Elena's. Banged on her door quiet.

She opened it quick. She looked about ten years older but apart from that she was stonking, only a bit haggard about the mince pies where she'd been leaking. And she looked thinner already about the cheeks as if she lost her appetite just thinking.

I went in and she shut the door. 'Please come in,' she went kind of dull. 'Please sit down.'

'Don't mind if I do Elena.'

She took a quick peek out the window then she drew the curtains closed.

'You will have tea.'

'Fair enough.'

She got the tea and then she got the vodka beside it. Opened a full bottle. Poured it out in two little glasses. Kind of solid sparkly glasses. I clocked some like them in the store. Probably she got towels and knickers and washing up bowls in the bargain like I clocked.

She sat down. Picked up her full glass. Put it down her throat.

'Good health,' she went. 'Bottoms up.'

'Yeah, cheers Elena, up your neck girl.'

'I hope you are enjoying Lithuania,' she turned round and went polite.

'Apart from being so cold so my short and curlies got the

162

mange, apart from that it seems right pukka Elena, know what I mean?'

She looked kind of doubtful about that. 'I will of course show you round the city,' she went.

'Oh, no need for that mate, got enough on your plate innit?'

'It is my duty as your host.'

'Well fair enough then.'

'But first we must talk, yes?'

'Just a bit yeah.'

'You must forgive me if my English is not so good. It is a long time since I was speaking it.'

'Your English is bleeding brilliant mate. You pick it up off the videos or what?'

'I was ballet dancer. When the Russians were here. We learned English for the ballet. Then I toured with the company. I joined the Bolshoi.'

'Bolshy, yeah, I heard of them.'

'Bolshoi. You are familiar with the ballet?'

'Not very familiar Elena. Not what you'd call close. Not much call for ballet round Walthamstow. I could work on it though, take in a spot of the old tap dancing, Fred Astaire and that.'

'Only three Lithuanians were chosen to go to the Bolshoi in Moscow. I was one. They sent us round the world. All Lithuanians learned Russian at school then, but they taught us English before we went to London and New York. Also I was in Chicago and Montreal.'

'Hope London was best.'

'London was very nice. I lived in Hackney.'

'Hackney? Was nice?'

'Very nice. I ate much curry. Very good for the dance.'

'Glad to be hearing it.'

'Tell me now why you are here Mr Burkett please.'

'Nicky.'

'Nicky. Tell me why you have come here to tell me that Jonas is dead.'

I gave her the gist. The history. Told her about me and Jimmy Foley stood standing in the dole queue when old Jonas got stuck. Told her how he turned round and said Elena then his plugs were pulled. She had a little weep again then, got to go in the bathroom for a natural. Then she came back and sat down and I told her the next bit. About the package. And how I got it with me.

She stared.

'Package?' she went. 'Is like a . . . parcel?'

'Little parcel yeah.'

She started bouncing up and down.

'You have it here?'

'Tell you about it in a minute girl. You got to be patient or I lose my thread. Got to finish the story first.'

She went something in Lithuanian. Or maybe Russian. Kind of nearly hysterical. Something on the lines of what the fuck's this bastard running on about when he got a parcel from my Jonas here probably.

'Oh my goodness,' she went in English. How they taught them in the ballet no doubting.

So I carried on about the shooting on Church Hill and the whacking the DI. Good story only she never seemed so interested in that part. In between told her about Noreen and me opening her parcel.

Then I told her what was in it.

Then pulled it out my jacket.

'WHAT!' she went.

'All yours Elena innit?'

'You have been walking in Vilnius all the time with this!'

'Course.'

'Oh God.'

'No reason not to, know what I mean?'

She took the package off me. Opened it. Clocked the necklace. Put it through her fingers. It was sparkling there. Then she started leaking all over again.

She touched the passport. Opened it. Checked it. Looked at the outside of the package, the name and address. Screwed up her boat and did some thinking.

'Of course I am not Elena Basanavicius,' she goes.

'No?'

'He is Jonas Basanavicius. I am Elena Sala. He wrote down Basanavicius I am thinking in case of emergency so that anyone should be sure about me. Like you.'

'Smart geezer.'

She held that passport in her fingers and she stared. She picked up that necklace and put it on her neck. Kind of absent minded. Then still absent minded she poured out more vodka and kind of absent minded she knocked it back. For being polite I did the same thing. All the time she fingered that passport.

Then she clocked me straight on.

'Why did you come here Mr Nicky?' she went.

'Nicky.'

'Nicky. Why did you come with this to Lithuania to tell me about Jonas?'

'Noreen spoked Elena. Sent me like. Kind of a sentimental bird. Then in the bargain your Jonas he gave me the trust innit? Carry out his wishes? Only I got to admit I was likely for not giving a toss about his wishes except for Noreen being around. Hard woman Elena.'

'Excuse me. Noreen is your wife? Your girlfriend?'

'My bird.'

'Your bird?'

'Like a girlfriend Elena only not so regular.'

'Ah. And she is sympathetic?'

'Always very sympathetic mate. Except to me.'

'And you did not tell the police about this?'

'Nah.'

'I see. I think.'

'I got a few problems with Old Bill in the past see.'

'Old Bill? Who is he?'

'Er . . . like police. Few problems. On account of they locked me up a few times. In them prisons.'

'You are criminal?'

'Well, in a manner of speaking Elena you put it like that. I did a few bits and bobs. Used to. Till I met bleeding Noreen I'm telling you, she won't be doing with all them bits of work like. I got to give up my way of life after I met up Noreen. Thing of the past. I ought to be stuffed in a museum.'

'She is very beautiful this Noreen?'

I thought about it.

'Matter of fact Elena yeah she very beautiful. That ain't half the problem though.'

'She is wonderful cook?'

I cackled. 'Nah, Noreen hardly boil a piece of yam. I does the cooking round our way. And the cleaning. Noreen only makes the decisions. All she does I'm telling you. Oh and earns the dosh what I don't get my mitts on much of.'

'You do cooking? Is it she decides what you cook as well? So how she makes these decisions, she has this control? You are a man!'

'Reckon I just got to be scared of her Elena.' I cackled. No explaining Noreen to any geezer. Or bird. Meet her was the only way for understanding her. She was one off the block.

She poured us more vodka.

'Now I tell you,' she went, 'why I am thinking Jonas gave you his passport.'

'Yeah?' I was getting kind of blurry from the vodka. 'You reckon the passport got to be important?'

'I think so. But first I tell you a little bit more about other things.'

We drank that vodka and she poured us another one.

NINETEEN

FIRST THOUGH SHE got up and peeked through the curtains.

She turned round and said something rude in Lithuanian.

'They back?' I went.

'They are back.'

'Being who?'

'Once they were friends.'

'Not now. They them gangsters?'

'Yes.'

'You tell them from their windows?'

'Yes. In Lithuania there are two peoples with black

windows in their cars. Either they are police. Or they are Mafia. Their cars are Mercedes or, how do you say . . . four-wheel drive?'

'Got you.'

'Well, these are gangsters.'

'How I'm thinking.'

'Jonas was gangster.'

'Correct.'

'He had to leave this country. There was gangster problem. It was, we say, overcrowding.'

'Too many gangsters?'

'Exactly. There were too many gangsters. When the Russians left the gangsters moved in. We already had our own gangsters. There were too many. They fought. Each one wanted the territory.'

'Drugs?'

'Drugs, yes. And cars and businesses. Nightclubs. There were battles. It became so some people had to leave. It was like, you know, lemmings?'

'I seen the TV. Go off a cliff?'

'Exactly. But they went to Warsaw or Berlin or London.'

'Same difference.'

'They flew.'

'Only they set up their business there in the bargain, am I right?' I got that bit off the DI about the Lithuanians. Before the Lithuanians whacked him.

'Yes. I think so. But I think then there were more troubles.'

'Same geezers. Same problems as back home. Too many came over. Wanted all the Lithuanian business. Territory.'

'Yes. There was not enough money for everyone. And here in Vilnius there was not enough money also. The country became more quiet. Gangsters were not so popular.'

'Old Bill again. Got their toes in.'

'The police began to be successful yes. But also the government did not like gangsters. They did not take the money. And the people too were against us. So you see there was not enough work here in Vilnius for Jonas and there were the other problems. Then there was not enough work in London. And there were same other problems.'

'Getting the picture.'

'There were many pressures on him. From many people.'

'So he got to be a grass.'

'Excuse me?'

'He got to be a grass Elena. He went to the Old Bill. Gave them baggage.'

'Pardon?'

'He told them police about them other gangsters.'

'No!'

'True words.'

'Oh God. You are sure? Jonas Basanavicius he became a, how you say, gas?'

'Grass.'

'Žolé?'

'More than likely.'

'I do not understand. Why did he do that? How did he become a žolé?'

'Dosh Elena. No other word for it.'

'Dosh? There is no other word? What does it mean?'

'Er, money Elena. Notes. Lettuce. Bits of folding paper like.'

'Money . . .'

'You already turned round and said it Elena. He got no work. And no dosh. So you want to know why he became a žolé, he needed the spends innit?'

'Innit?' she goes.

'What I'm thinking, see, Elena, is he knew a lot. Old Bill they're very, very uppity indeed about old Jonas getting stiffed. More than just him being a grass. Normal they never be arsed over a grass getting whacked. But they're all in a proper tizz over this one. So I reckon not only he knew a bagful, there's something more. Maybe he was a big tiddler. Kind of involved. Maybe he got something both sides is wanting. Dunno what. Only both lots is very fucking keen on following up even after he got the full message. And it ain't never this necklace you got they're wanting, not the way I'm thinking.'

Elena sat back in her chair. She was clocking me and she was thinking. Her little beadies screwed right up and her forehead got locked in a trench.

'Nicky you have some more vodka,' she went. She poured it out. I did as I was told.

'I am having an idea,' she turned round and said.

'Good girl Elena,' I went. 'Carry on sis.' I was sort of starting falling asleep there. It was hot in her flat and the way she was pouring out the vodka was never making it any colder.

'I think it was very important that you bring the passport,' she goes.

'Yeah?'

'There was a reason.'

'Yeah?'

'I know that reason what it was.'

'No problem Elena, know what I mean?'

I started on a little kip in her chair.

'Would you like to dip your wick?' Elena asked.

I woke up very sudden. Least I thought I was awake. I nearly fell off my chair. I snorted. I coughed.

'Excuse me?' I went.

'Do you want to dip your wick with me?'

'Elena,' I turned round and said. 'You reckon what that means?'

'As you know I was in London few times,' she went explaining. 'And I am ballet dancer.'

Ballet dancers always were goers so I heard.

'Stands to reason,' I went non-committal.

'I heard about dipping your wick.'

'What it is?'

'All the men dancers in England,' she goes. 'They always spoke of dipping their wick. Usually with each other.'

'Ah.'

'So how do you yourself call it, the sex act?'

'Well, me and Noreen like, we generally turn round and say you fancy a touch of howsyourfather or what?'

'Howsyourfather?'

'When we call it anything like. Most often tell the truth we just do it. Bosh.' I was rambling. I was kind of smacked in the gob.

She poured more vodka. 'Do you ever call it making love?'

'Well, yeah, course. Making love, know what I mean?'

'Nicky, do you want to make love with me?'

It got to be that propriating again. When you got death you got to get life. Couldn't wait to tell Noreen about it. Second thoughts maybe not.

'It is such a long time since I am having sex. Because of what happens I am badly needing it even more now than before.'

I could sympathise with that. We drank our vodka and thought about it all.

She poured more. 'I need it now Nicky,' she went. She stood there kind of beautiful, looking down brave and leaking.

The way she put it, it was kind of a public service. Probably get it on the national health. I was like a doctor.

She took me by the hand and she led me up her bedroom. It was all very quiet in there. She got the deepest duvet in England.

Except we were never in England. Were we? I was trying to think.

Then her bedroom got soft lights and they were going round and round. So was I. I crashed against the door post. I crashed against the bed post. Then I crashed into her duvet. I knew I was getting unconscious. I thought it best I had a little snooze.

When I woke up Elena was bringing me the smallest cup of coffee you ever saw. Except it was in a glass. And no vodka.

She smiled at me kind of sad. And kind of smirky. 'That was very nice,' she turned round and said.

Was it? What was?

Did we do it?

I got clothes on. I kind of had a feel round, see if I felt like I just did it or what. No fucking idea.

'Yeah,' I went grinning at her happy. 'Very nice Elena, kind of smashing, know what I mean?' Couldn't exactly ask her the situation. Not quite good manners, yeah, glad you had a good time, er, did we do it?

'Now we must be busy,' she went. 'Before the post office closes.'

'Post office? You want to send a postcard? Cash a giro?'

'I think the men in the motor car have gone for today. They will return in the morning. If they see you here again they will watch all the time. We must go to the post office now.'

'Fair enough Elena. Fair enough girl. You want me to come with you or what?'

'You must come with me.'

'No problem mate.'

'You will be Jonas Basanavicius.'

'Who?'

'Jonas.'

'Who me? Jonas?'

'We will be changing your picture. Then we will go. We have one hour until the post office it shuts. If the men do not come back we must go tonight.'

I never had a clue what she was going on about. But she pointed me in her shower and I wakened up and she gave me three more glasses of black coffee side by side on the table. I sat down and took them while she messed with our passports. Jonas's and mine.

It was all a bit sudden. Me, I was all in favour of not getting too sentimental after a quick one. Get up and carry on as normal. On the other hand this was a bit trickier. Did we get a quick one? Were we getting up and carrying on as normal because we got it or because we never? Was she a hard bird or was she a scorned woman?

Then again there was the vodka. Plus the kip. Plus the cold outside. It was all a bit difficult.

On the other subject, I reckoned I was innocent until proved guilty. That was my statement anyhow.

TWENTY

'You see,' she turned round and said.
  'Trying Elena.'
'Something is in the post office for Jonas.'
'Yeah?'
'They put a paper in my door. An information that a parcel is there.'
'Yeah?'
'I did not collect it. I cannot because it is his name. So I wait. Then you bring the passport.'
'Yeah?'
'For collecting a parcel from the post office you are needing a passport.'

'Yeah?' It was starting to dawn.

'No other document is good. They will not accept any identity except passport.'

'Ah . . .'

'So you see, Jonas he knew there was parcel waiting for me.'

'You reckon he sent that parcel?'

'He wanted that I should have the parcel. Very badly he wanted it. He knew' – she blew a bit, looked away – 'he knew when he was in front of you he was not coming himself. So he gave to you his passport.'

'Trusted me like.'

'Yes. In one way. I do not think he expected you to come yourself.'

'He was never knowing Noreen.'

'Probably he was hoping you put the passport in the post box. It is for this reason it was addressed. He did not think you are opening it.'

'Er, yeah. Fact he probably trusted me not to peek, seeing it that way.'

'Yes.'

'Pity.'

'Never mind. It is done. And I am glad that you came.' She gave me a big beamer. One moment I reckoned she was nearly blushing. Whatever we did. Or didn't.

'Yeah, er, me too Elena.'

She was making herself busy with the passport. Mine

and his. Been at it half an hour when I kipped and showered. Now she looked up happy. There it was.

There it was. Jonas Basanavicius, born and bred Lithuanian out of East London. All his details on it, only my mug was different. Sealed and delivered.

I was about to be Jonas.

Only I reckoned there might be one bit missing in her plan.

'You teach me a few words Elena?' I went. 'About the weather and that? Before we go in their post office and start yacking?'

'I shall do all the talking,' she turned round and said. 'You shall be standing only. To be Jonas. They do not know him because we only move here one year ago and then he was straight away in London. I tell them he works away. You will be Jonas for them but you shall not speak.'

'Fair enough girl.'

She went round the windows again clocking the manor from the side. No dark motors. She got her woollies on. I got my extra strides and the rest. On top she got her coat and hat.

Then she gave me the tourist gangster rundown.

'Uzupis,' she went, 'is not gangster district.'

'No?'

'We came to Uzupis,' she carried on explaining, 'because there are not gangsters here. We had already problems with other gangsters. Uzupis is artistic district. It was quite

181

dirty district before, painters and writers and students and actors. Now we are making it new. Clean people like us came in. It becomes fashion place to live. Vilnius is becoming new. So is Uzupis.'

'Bleeding beautiful you ask me Elena got to say. Whole of the manor.'

'I think so. Now we go.'

We took a good butcher's from the start. Stepped out her door, checked the stairs. Went out in her yard, looked out all the recesses. Went over to the gateway only never went on the street till we searched it careful. Then we went through the arch and on the pavement. Turned left.

Post office was only a couple of minutes up, on the next street called Kriviu. All their post offices got a number, Elena turned round and said. You got to collect your parcels at your local number. Kriviu was 2007. Marked on the building. We got there. Stopped, breathed in, opened the door and went in. Her in front.

It was kind of like a hallway more than a room. It was dusty. They got a counter there and behind it they got three biddies doing their knitting. The staff never wanted to be disturbed. Bad day for sending a postcard.

Elena blew in there like a princess. She waved, she laughed, she smelled good. She yacked away to the biddies about their knitting and their post office and maybe their kids and their grandkids and women's problems and the weather and shoes. She never stopped. Seemed her idea was she yacked all the time and they never noticed I was a dumbo. Under the thumb.

The biddies had a minor thaw. Icicles dropped off their fangs. Frost started to melt.

She carried on yacking. Now about me, pointed me up, telling how I just came home to her after working away. One of the biddies nearly smiled. Romance for you. Elena took the passport out of my mitt, laid it on the counter. Carried on burbling. They carried on sitting. She carried on still yacking. Then a pause came along.

It was like the earth stopped.

One of them got up very, very slowly. She put her mitts on her hips and she groaned and she struggled and she panted. She lifted up her back, she bent her knees. She stood.

When she was upright she paused for considering the world from this new angle. Seemed she found it mainly to her approval, give or take. She stretched. She shuffled over to the back room.

She went in there.

Total silence. No-one turned round and said a dickie.

Suspense. Several minutes.

Maybe the lady died out there. Maybe she was dead before she even went.

Then she cried out back there.

'Taip!' she went.

She found something.

183

There was a rumbling and a stumbling and she was on her way back. She came round the doorway. Kind of exhausted. Grinning. Triumphant.

She was making motions back towards me. Eventual she reached up the counter. She was carrying a parcel. It seemed like a large carrier bag wrapped in fancy paper with a label on it.

The fancy paper was from Harrod's in London. They wrapped it up for Jonas.

The biddy put it on the counter. Then she waited a moment panting. Then she picked up my passport, least Jonas's passport with my pic inside.

She clocked the outside of it. Then she pushed it further away. Then further. Then it was far enough away for her to be reading it, only by that time the writing was too small for her. She gave up. Never even clocked the inside. Waste of time changing the photos.

She passed a piece of paper over. Elena got a pen already in her hand. She coached me before on Jonas's signature. As it goes though it never mattered on account of the biddy never looked at this neither.

She gave me the parcel.

We bibbed and we bobbed. We grinned at them. We wished them all the laba dienas we could think of except mine were all silent ones. We wished them a lot of other things I never understood. Two of the biddies smiled this time.

We took the parcel and we turned round slowly and we went to their door like geezers never got a care in the world. We went back on the street.

We had another clock round. Nobody. We walked a few seconds back downhill towards her gaff.

I couldn't hold it.

'Drugs?' I went.

'No. I do not think so. Please keep your voice quiet.'

'Oh yeah course. Forgot and that.' I was too excited.

We went quiet back to her house and then we went upstairs to her flat. No grief anywhere.

When we opened that parcel though we reckoned there might be grief arriving quite very soon. Or even sooner than that.

TWENTY-ONE

IT WAS VERY very large quantities.
   Of twenty pound notes.
And fifty pound notes.
Used.
'Jesus H. fucking Johnson,' I went.
'It is money,' she went. And she was quite right.

It was hard to turn round and say how much there was. I never clocked so much lettuce. The three large ones the DI gave over in the boozer looked like small change, what you send your kid down the corner with for a paper and a packet of rizlas.

I was trying to count it without looking like I was counting it.

She took it in the bedroom. Tipped it all on the bed.

She started cackling.

She lay on it. She started rolling in it.

She kicked her legs in the air.

Then she got up and started counting.

It was all tied up with elastic bands how they do it in the bank. Only this time it was never in even amounts. Maybe he was going to do it when he got home, unfortunate he got stiffed first. All the different bundles made it hard to count.

Still I knew five scores made a century. Ten scores made a double. Fifty scores made a large one even though I never fingered all that in one go. And if fifty twenties made a large one, twenty fifties made a large one in the bargain.

I got a packet in my hand. Worked a bundle of twenties to about a grand, then a bundle of fifties.

Harrod's bags were a handy size for the job. Probably they made them like that so the upper classes could carry their dosh in them.

Jonas was never the most successful villain in the world. Successful villains were more in the alive area. On the other hand he got a bit of a result in some ways, something to show for his career plan. All this paper never could be total Old Bill money. Maybe five, maybe ten. Top whack was twenty or even twenty-five for high profile nickings, big faces behind bars. Not worth it for twenty-five you might turn round and say. True it meant you never got nicked yourself. Looked at that way maybe twenty-five was a bargain. Trouble was though you spent the rest of your days looking over your shoulder for dying. Tricky decision.

But this was mega money. Jonas got this from other sources not Old Bill.

More than likely some of it was the legit product of villainy. His own villainy. Robbing and thieving and that.

Some of it on the other hand was maybe the product of someone else's villainy. Which might account for how some geezers somewhere might be thinking they wanted it back.

And just for the aggravation maybe they reckoned they take their own money back plus Jonas's legit money from his villainy plus the dosh he got from Old Bill for grassing them up.

Which by my counting was totalling over a hundred thousand pound notes.

'Jesus H. fucking Johnson,' I went again.

Now I knew what they meant by rolling in it. She was taking all the elastic bands off and scattering it all over the bed. And laughing. Laughing and rolling, rolling and laughing.

Then she started taking her clothes off.

Then she got up and she pulled me down with her and then before I could turn round and say Jack Robinson, except I was never thinking about turning round and

189

saying Jack Robinson, she was taking my clothes off in the bargain.

It was very warm in there admittedly and I still got most my clothes on for outside. So she took one of my pairs of trousers off, much more comfortable.

In the bargain she took one of her pairs of. Except she was only wearing one.

It was all getting very interesting. I always heard how dosh made birds horny. Get your BMW and you got a bit of wobbly trotting off the estate. Buy your castle up Loughton with the footballers and big mixers, what happens only you got a blonde attached. Only I never heard about wanting it in it.

Lithuanians seemed keen on a touch in my experience.

It was all getting very interesting. Sort out the question once for all if we did it or not the first time. See if we did it or not this time.

Then her telephone rang.

Dreadful pause.

We clocked each other.

Then she got up and she yacked in the other room in Lithuanian like there was no tomorrow.

When she came back she never got the same interest.

'This is for you Nicky,' she turned round and said. She handed over a bundle of notes. Almost made a dent in the mountain.

'Here Elena there ain't no need girl.'

'Yes of course there is need. You bring the passport because Jonas wanted you to do this. Of course he is also wanting you to have a per cent.'

'Fair enough girl. Fair enough.' I put the bundle in my pocket. Very sharp.

'Now you must go home tonight.'

'What?' Seemed like she got no further use for my services.

'I will go with you as far as Germany.'

'Yeah?'

'I cannot exchange this money here. Perhaps a little. I can exchange it in Germany. There are many banks. No-one knows. And also I must leave the country quickly. I am thinking now we will go into the city as if for dinner. But we will catch the train.'

'Yeah?' All going a bit fast for me. 'Elena, my ticket ain't for two days. What Noreen turned round and said, I got to go on that special train or I lose all my dosh.'

'This is not your big problem.'

'No?'

'You have seen you have much money in your pockets now.'

'True.'

'It is your problem if they find you with this money. And it is a problem if they kill you. I think it is important that we should leave tonight.'

'Seeing it your way Elena maybe you got a point there.'

'We will leave very soon. I must make some calls on the telephone. My sister will look after my apartment when I am not here. Perhaps you will take a shower while you are waiting.'

'Yeah, er, all right mate.' I went off in the bathroom.

I had a shower. Then seeing as how I got time to kill I took a butcher's in her cupboards.

She got a can of shaving foam with the top off. Disposable razor beside it. Spare toothbrush. Spare hairbrush.

Maybe they were Jonas's bits and bobs left over. Or maybe Elena was shaving her legs. And brushing them.

Or maybe life was more complicated than I reckoned and I better be watching my back.

TWENTY-TWO

'WE WILL NOT TAKE the aeroplane,' she announced coming in the bathroom with black tea for me.

'Correct,' I went, on account of she already turned round and said we were going on the chuffer.

But it seemed like she was more sure after she made the calls.

'They will expect us to take the aeroplane. It is easier to go quietly on the train.'

'Slower.'

'And it is more quiet to buy a ticket. So now we go to a restaurant. Then we go to your hotel. We take your case and we go to the station.'

'Round the corner innit?'

'Exactly.'

'No problem getting a ticket Elena? They ain't sold out already?'

'I have made a telephone call. People that I know will arrange a ticket. It will be held for us.'

'Fair enough girl.'

Then we picked up all our dosh and we packed it round our bodies. Wearing two pairs of strides I got plenty pockets. Then it went in my bum bag and my shirt and my jacket and my boots. I was packed. As a bonus it made more layers. Keep all my bits warm and cosy. Elena went in the bathroom, then she went in the bedroom, then she came out looking bigger than she went in.

'You looking kind of busty Elena,' I went. 'Drive a geezer wild you hear me?'

'Shut up,' she went. Mind on other matters. Starting to feel kind of tense maybe. 'I am thinking now about our trip only,' she goes.

'Fair enough girl. One thing at a time eh?'

She got one small bag. Put it over her shoulder. Picked up her keys. She got about seventeen keys for all her locks. We went out the door and she did the business. We turned to go down.

Geezer was coming up the stairs. Very big, dark geezer. He was never saying anything.

She shot him.

He fell back down the stairs. She got a handgun in her bag. When she clocked him she put her mitt in the bag and she never even took the shooter out, only whacked him through the canvas.

'Jesus fuck,' I went.

Ballet dancers could surprise you sometimes.

We went down the stairs. Geezer was panting a bit. He was still alive except you could never turn round and say he sounded healthy. He was lying off on one side. We went past him and we went out.

I hoped he was a villain. I hoped he never came round for selling insurance.

On the other hand, if he was Jehovah's Witness he got what he deserved.

Problems never stopped there though. Whatever the fuck he was, unlikely he was on his tod. Probably there was more of them on the street. Jehovah's Witnesses or insurance sellers or gangsters. Waiting for their mate or for us.

We went out bold as you like. Or trying. Elena was shaking. I was shaking like a widget. We went across the yard and out on the road.

Up the hill and across the street was the Merc with tinted windows.

We turned the other way and went down the hill towards the river.

We heard a door open in the motor. Never turned

round. Let them be thinking. Maybe we passed their man on the stairs. Maybe it was never us. Maybe he was having a sit down somewhere.

No footsteps after us. No door shutting neither. Got to be some geezer was still stood standing. We carried on shanking. I could hear my legs wobbling.

Already where we reached they needed a good shooter for the distance. Like a rifle. Still we carried on down the hill. Then we went round the corner and we were out of sight. We never speeded up even though I was wanting to fuck off like a dust storm.

'Shit,' I went breathing out.

Elena was gasping.

'You planning on shooting any more parties?' I went.

She was still gasping, heaving.

'You heard how it makes some big geezers kind of irritable when you plug their squaddies?'

'We go to restaurant.'

'Spot of pizza line the old stomach right nice.'

She started leaking. Natural reaction in a woman, bit of stress and that.

Unfortunate I started leaking in the bargain. Extra unfortunate on account of my tears started freezing on my boat race. How I heard it, you got salt in your tears and they put salt on the roads to stop it freezing when it was freezing. So tears they never ought to be freezing. Maybe I got to eat more salt. Suffering from deficiency. Probably my mum's fault. Anyhow my tears were fucking freezing all down my fucking hooter.

Not good for you rep, standing there blubbing.

Next to a murderer, blubbing in the bargain. Or an attempted murderer.

Me wondering how it was she gave me some great wodge of spends and never shot me, when she shot some geezer maybe came to clean the drains. I rated the old charm factor high only not that high. Maybe it was returning a favour. Or maybe it was fucking nothing of the sort, more like she was on her tod in a spot of grief and even when she belled her mates she never got no assist coming over the hill. Yet.

We walked across the bridge. I scraped off the tears like a lollipop now. We were both waddling. Elena was carrying a fucking sight more dosh than me and she was about three sizes bigger than usual. One advantage she got to be near as bullet proof.

Over the bridge and we back in the city. They were never finding us there except by accident or they knew where I was dozing or they waited for us at the station.

Or Elena she warned up some other lot already. Whosit.

'We go for a pizza then or what?' I went.

'We will eat a pizza now, yes.'

Big pizza gaff was down the square not far off their Town Hall. Full of young people. You wanted to shoot a geezer in there you got to take out a gaggle of students in the bargain. Ill wind type of thing.

They never heard about the extra chillies in Lithuania yet. I got the mushrooms instead. Last time I ate mushrooms was when Noreen got ideas. I hoped no-one got any ideas in the restaurant.

Maybe that accounted for my nerves shaking. I was wobbling so much I could never hardly get that pizza down my neck.

She leaned close over the table and she gave me the gaze. Uh-oh. It was time for the personals. Never mind she just shot a geezer.

All birds were the same. Give them any little touch of the familiars and next thing they wanted the full cell interview. Usually stated with a chat about your ex-birds.

Not this time though.

'Tell me about yourself Nicky,' she went.

'Oh Gawd.'

This was where it went towards the birds, after the one about yourself.

'Your mother, were you very close to her?'

'Eh?'

'Family life we believe it is very important.'

'Innit?'

'It begins with the birth, the closeness.'

'For definite I got birthed Elena. Not too sure how close it was.'

'Was there feeding with the breast?'

'Do me a favour Elena,' I went. Thought of my mum and all that. 'They got bottles, know what I mean?'

'Here in Lithuania they have bottles now. But I believe it does not help family life. You have many sisters and brothers?'

I reckoned maybe she never helped family life for the geezer she just wasted. Still best for not pointing that out. 'Yeah I got Sharon my sis,' I goes. 'Enough for anyone.'

'You are close to her?'

'She ain't too bad I suppose considering.'

'I have one sister. We are very close.'

'Fair enough girl.' I was hoping that was the end of it.

'You have children?'

Jesus. 'Yeah I got Danny the boy. Chip off the block. No messing with Danny. Does that judo and karate and tai chi and feng shui and hara-kiri, you name it he got belts in it.'

'I have no children.'

'Good on yer Elena.'

'Yet.'

Oops.

'I have need for children. They will be ballet dancers.'

'Fair enough.'

'They have close families.'

199

Least Danny was never likely for being a ballet dancer then.

'And strong legs.'

'No doubting Elena. All that twirling. Fair enough girl.'

'You have strong legs.'

'No!' Came out louder than I expected. 'Very weak Elena. Very feeble, kind of a puff of wind type.'

'Do you have any, how do you say, inhibitions?'

'Yes! No!'

'Or maybe you have some good strong cousins. Your family, they are very extended?'

'Tell the truth Elena most of them are a bit on the short side.'

'Would you like a pudding?'

I was confused by now. All the rabbiting, I was never sure the pudding was part of her game plan.

'No thanks Elena,' I went. 'Not the day for a pudding, give me the cobbly wobblies, know what I mean?'

She went ahead though. Her digestion not upset by shootings or yacking about babies, both did their effect on me. Very hard woman. She got a pistachio ice.

I was confused about Elena. Shootings or babies, you never wanted to keep your back turned.

TWENTY-THREE

S AME GEEZER WAS still on the desk at the hotel.
　'All right mate?' I went.
　'All right mate?' he went.
　Elena came in and sat in the lobby.
　'Ah, you have found nice Lithuanian girl,' he turned round and said.
　'Ballet dancer.'
　'They were always the best.'
　We could yack on geezer to geezer, only I got to do the business. 'Look Boris,' I goes.
　'Yes?'

'Very sorry and that only I got to be making my moves now. All kind of unexpected, no offence it just too fucking parky here, know what I mean? Freeze the cobblers off an icicle. You keep the dosh for the room, welcome to it, only I got to be going home.'

'With her?'

'Nah mate. On my tod. She only for decoration innit?'

Elena fidgeting. Maybe sat in an uncomfortable chair.

'I just came in for getting my clobber then I got to be off.'

'Yes? You take the train?'

'Got a lift. To Moscow.'

'Moscow? You have a ride to Moscow?'

'In a truck.'

'A truck? You are very lucky. What kind of a truck?'

'Waste disposal.'

'Ah?'

'See ya.' I went upstairs with the key. No trusting any geezer now. I checked the door where I taped it. No problem. Went inside and still checked round in case they came in the windows. No problem. I bagged up my gear and got out again sharpish.

And we were gone.

Round the corner and across the street was their train station, just where it was when I came in. We got half an hour before the train left. Elena already had the words about our tickets. Now we picked them up and paid the dosh. All seemed easier when you spoke the lingo. And paid the backhander probably. We sat on a bench and clocked the bookings together.

'We not in the same sleeper?' I went.

'No. It is not permitted.'

'Shit. I was kind of thinking that trains give a bit of legup for a spot of romancing, know what I mean?' As it goes it was a fucking relief though. Strain of deciding whether we did it for real or not was getting kind of heavy.

'I know what you mean.' She put her bonce down one moment and I could swear she gave a little blush. What this meant either way though was another mystery. Women. 'But you will notice that there are compartments for men and there are compartments for women on the train. There is no intercourse.'

'Innit?'

It was the train for Warsaw. I already knew from Noreen it was easier getting back home not going by Minsk. And thank fuck for that. Overnight for Warsaw then change for Berlin then change for Cologne. It was like fucking history books and geography rolled into one. All it needed was a few battles and the Gulf Stream.

'Warsaw,' I went a bit unbelieving, although being my second time now it ought to be like Hoe St.

'We will arrive there at 5.47 in the morning.'

Kind of unbelieving about that in the bargain.

'Then we will take the 6.45 for Berlin.'

'Fair enough Elena.'

'Here are your tickets. Keep them very safe.'

'Innit.'

We got a coffee and lurked. Elena seemed kind of happy to be with me. I wondered she was on my side or not. Out of ten I reckoned it was about six and a half. Course I was never too sure which side I was on neither, mine or someone else's. Then again I wondered who the fuck else might be on my side, whichever side that was, or on the opposite or backwards. Then I wondered they got the news we were on the chuffer.

One thing, a train was kind of easier to jump off than a plane if it got warm. But it lasted longer. Either way I'd be a fucking sight cheerier when I was tucked up tight in Walthamstow. The fuck I was doing here was more of a fucking puzzler every moment. I made a point I never wanted to do anything like this more. Point of principle.

Except the dosh was even bigger. I patted my pockets.

They stood standing by their carriages like a stagecoach, riding shotgun. Smarter geezers than my Russian mates on the last one. Unfortunate they were all geezers though so no hope of a touch off some smart uniformed bird round midnight.

'All right mate?' I went to my geezer. We found our

carriages Elena's and mine.

'Kphshtchlh,' he went.

'How I was thinking.'

'They are Polish,' went Elena.

'Nah. I reckoned they was Australian.'

'Shut up,' she went. 'And do not talk to them in the train. Do not talk to anyone.'

'Fair enough girl. Only trying for the old culturals, know what I mean? Spot of chat, couple of lagers and swap knives type of thing.'

'You are keeping quiet. Until Germany. Then it might be safe and you may conduct yourself in any arsehole way that you want.'

She picked up some good words in that ballet. Remember to keep my Danny away from their dancing classes case he got corrupted.

'Yeah I was forgetting Elena. Quiet as a banker now me. Never even clock me scratching.'

'I will see you in Warsaw. Have a nice trip.'

Very nice trip yeah. Full of highlights. Be dark all the way so nothing to clock out of the window. All I got left to read was my guide to Vilnius, a brochure of the holocaust museum and the bible I nicked out of the hotel. Be lucky I never threw myself under the fucking train. I got a hunk of bread and some cheese and a tin of beans I brought from home, never go outside the borough without a tin of beans. I forgot the spoon though, could be tricky. I got a bottle of water. And I got to kip on a bunk. Nice trip yeah.

Got a result on the bunk all the same. I found the compartment and checked the ticket. Yes! Bottom bunk. No mountaineering. And no other geezer in the compartment it looked like.

I reckoned.

Guard came round. Checked my ticket. Checked my bunk.

'Phthshchzhski,' he went.

'Fair enough John,' I goes.

'Herbate kave,' he goes, pointing up his cubby hole down the corridor.

'Thank you geezer.' No fucking clue what he turned round and said only he seemed like he meant well. Check out his herbate kave later.

'No problem,' he goes. Showed his molars. Friendly geezer.

I started off taking out a couple of things for the night. Toothbrush and vodka. Cheese and bread. Beans. Brochure of the holocaust museum. The train started off. Just when it juddered a small commotion broke out. Outside door opened. Some geezer got in. Door shut again. I earholed the geezer yacking to the guard. They got different languages, one coughing and one sneezing. Seemed to understand each other. Couple of laughs. Then shuffles came down the corridor. Shuffling and snuffling.

Sounded like a bear.

It was a bear.

Huge geezer blocked the doorway. Been a sun, he'd block it out in the bargain. Huge and hairy. Coat big as a tent. Skin like a fox. Neck like a tree. Eyebrows made barbed wire look soft. Feet like a yeti. He was two people in one.

'All right mate?' I went weak.

He gave me the gaze.

He clocked me up and down. Then he clocked my beans. He raised his barbed wire. He bent over like a building folding and he picked the beans up. I reckoned maybe he was wanting to gob them. Without opening the tin. He picked them off my bunk. Then he put them on the top bunk.

Then my cheese and bread. And toothbrush and vodka.

And my bag.

He was indicating he preferred me to sleep upstairs. If I never minded too much.

'Fair enough Ivan,' I turned round and said. 'As it goes I was only thinking of moving up there myself. Only saying to myself I was, how the view was bound to be better up there. Of the ceiling.'

He never dickied a word. It was obvious we were going to get on like mates. We never argued.

Then he went out in the corridor again. When he went to the side of the train I felt it lean over.

I went upstairs. I gobbed my cheese and bread no

problem and my beans tipped them up down the hole. I drank water and vodka. I stared up the ceiling. Then I went to kip.

Before the murder.

It was 4.50 on my clock. Unless you were out clubbing or thieving or you got a condition you were supposed to be sleeping.

Ivan downstairs was nodding nicely. He was yacking in his sleep. He was never very happy about something. He was grunting and swearing and roaring. Maybe some geezer got his bunk. Then he was snoring loud enough for a football crowd.

I was awake. There was no fucking question about me sleeping. When he started on yacking I was awake and then when he started on snoring I was awaker. I was never going back to kip. He was laying on his front snoring into the pillow. I lay there thinking about murdering him. Sticker in the back. Even that probably never quieten him down.

Door slid open. We already got our visitation off the border Old Bill hours before so it was never them. Some geezer couldn't sleep maybe on account of the din. Speak soft to Ivan, pinch his nostrils.

One geezer came in. One more stood in the corridor.

Light came in from the corridor. In that light there was something flashing. It was a long thin sticker.

Geezer brought it down into the bunk below. Lined up, lifted it again and stuck it down hard.

Whoomph. Came from Ivan.

They stabbed him. Took their knife with them.

Then I remembered it was supposed to be me in that bottom bunk.

TWENTY-FOUR

I WAS OUT AND off and heading down the fucking corridor.

More than likely they were coming back. First do the business. Then fuck off out, case it never worked and he got irritable. Then come back for checking if he was moving or needed finishing. Maybe even checking they got the right geezer. When they clocked it was never a geezer from E17 they whacked I was keen to be some other place.

Down the end of the corridor they were stood standing.

I went the other way. Socks on, no shoes. I ran. Made for the guard's cubbyhole.

Door open. Not there.

Fuck and shit.

They were coming. Very noisy. Maybe they reckoned I was the geezer they stuck or maybe a witness, either way they were after. I ran, pulled doors open, headed for the next carriage. Stood one moment over the join in the carriages. Yanked the next door open. Shoved it shut behind.

I clocked our guard coming back, heard the trouble. Been having a vodka with his mate next door. I pushed past the other side of him. Yelled at him. Yelled nothing only sounds. He gaped. I ran on. They came past the two of them, knocked him out the way. I heard the thud. Ran on not looking back. Pulled another door open. Stood over another join in the carriages. Looked down. Looked up. Climb up? Nah. Open a door? Be dead. I ran in the next coach. The women's sleeper.

Some woman in the corridor was having a smoke. They were behind me, catching up. I ran past her then got her and pulled her round between us.

They stabbed her in the gut.

I was against the wall. She was between. They were gone. Back the way they came.

Oh dear.

The guards came. Mine coming back. The one from this coach. One from every coach. It was manic.

The woman slumped. She was gasping. Gasping but alive. This time they left the knife in.

No-one spoke English. Asked me a stack of questions.

Turned to the woman. A doctor appeared, passenger. Then Elena came. Spoke languages they understood.

It was still manic.

Through Elena I told them everything. Least everything they needed to know. Elena filled in bits. What she wanted. They never stopped the train. And they never found the geezers neither. I reckoned they chose nearly five o'clock on account of we were due in Warsaw at 5.47 so they could disappear. When we got there Old Bill came in numbers too late as usual.

We sat in their office up Warsaw station. Fucking six o'clock in the morning. They got the night manager in, spoke English. They asked about my journey. Asked what I clocked of events. Told them. I never got round to mention how it was me should have been on the bottom bunk. They never asked. Never spotted the reservation. Feller did some kind of deal with the guard for getting on the train, so it all got kind of blurred. Too much for Old Bill anyhow, it was the night shift caught the short straw and wanted to be home. Night shift probably the thick ones in the bargain. I told about the shafting then told how I ran off down the train into the birds' coach then how the woman bravely stepped between me and them. Protecting the foreign guest in her land got to be.

They reckoned the woman was going to live. Nice. Bit too poorly to be giving evidence just yet though.

213

The geezer in my bunk though he was never going to live. On account of he was dead. Two stabs with the sticker and he was dozing for ever. No more snoring. Seemed to me like another expert sticking, find the spot straight off.

Like old Jonas in the dole queue. Kind of a suspicious link.

Kind of like they never did it only to stop the snoring.

I told them how Elena being a passenger came out of her bunk on account of the din. She spoke Russian and English. Guards spoke Russian and Polish. Communicated. Good will. No problem. Guards never spotted a connection with us. Old Bill got no reason.

They took details. My name, address, birthday, passport, ticket, occupation (businessman), next of kin, scars, beauty spots. I was innocent bystander and I was very co-operative natural. Also traumatised. So they got no reason to keep me in their country. Best of luck and that. Maybe the Polish embassy in London be in touch. Maybe ask me back if they lifted the geezers and wanted me for witness.

They never searched me. No need. Innocent witness. Traumatised. They shook my mitt. I shook their mitts. Knew I got a train to catch. Thank you geezers. Mind if I go now? All right mate. Fact, best you fucked off soon as possible so we can sweep the grief under the carpet. Be swift, eh?

It was 6.37. I guessed it was the record fastest Old Bill investigation in Poland.

I walked out their office on to their platform.

Elena?

She was gone.

She was never there.

Fuck and shit. It was 6.37 in the fucking morning and I was in fucking Warsaw. Warsaw, Poland. Anything possible in this world might get worse?

Apart from starting with the same letter Warsaw got no fucking thing in common with Walthamstow at all. Except the next letter was the same in the bargain. I was there in Warsaw on my tod after clocking a murder and an attempted, the whole fucking batch was out for me, I was fucking starving and dying of thirst, all the words were seventeen letters long, it was doing my brain in and I was shitless.

But not potless.

Most important just then, I got Polish dosh left from my journey the other way. I looked up on their board. No point waiting around for fucking Elena. I got a very nasty feeling I was never clocking her mush again. Why? Fuck alone knew. Not mine to reason. Anyhow, wondering on my situation, catching a train in Polish got to be the same like catching a train in all the other fucking languages I went through. Only reason this time was I just witnessed another murder, no reason to get wound up. Their board reckoned it was train EC 46 to Berlin, only then before I even started searching out the platform there I clocked train EC 46 for Berlin stood standing right in front of me. Berlin thank fuck was the same in all the languages so I never even got to translate.

Coffee bar stood by the side. I went in. 'Coffee mate please,' I went. Just now I had enough of languages.

'Coffee?'

'Yeah mate. Big.' I made signs. He got my message. He passed it over quick. It was thick and it was black.

'Geezer, I reckon you just saved a feller's life,' I goes. Doshed him some paper out of the Polish packet. Never worried over the change. I was on that train like shit in a stream. Find my reserved place later.

I sat in the first seat came along. Drank the coffee. Went straight to kip. Got to be the trauma.

In moments I was miles away. Down the market drinking coffee and gobbing a couple of patties with Jimmy Foley. Back home.

TWENTY-FIVE

'TICKET!' WENT THE UNIFORM.

'YAAH!' I went.

'TICKET!' he went again unimpressed.

He was a big smart geezer shining off his uniform. Even his barnet shone. Even his hooter shone, got to be he polished it before he came to work.

'Mister you just woke me out of dreamland,' I goes. 'I reckoned for one moment you was German.'

He was German. It was a German train.

Now there was something about Germans and it was never even one of them was fucking my babymother Kelly. Deserved sympathy on that one. I met a bunch of

Germans. They came down Charlie Chan's where they went for the stabbing. Spectator sport for tourists, got a few lagers in, chat a few birds then come out in the car park after and clock the traditional custom of English stabbing each other. Go back home to Frankfurt and tell their mums and dads. I met them up Walthamstow market, longest street market in Europe, buy a sweet potato and a few moody Nikes for taking home. Then again I met them up West Ham, some reason all the Germans came down the Boleyn. And there you fucking got it. No matter who they were or where you met them, every German I ever met ran on all the time about how they fucking stuffed us in every fucking World Cup.

Almost every World Cup.

'WE WERE THERE IN 2001!' I went to their guard.

'TICKET!' he went.

'MICHAEL OWEN HAD SOME FUN.' Pity about Owen being a Scouser.

He yawned.

'EASY PEASY FIVE TO ONE!'

He grabbed the seat reservation out my mitt.

'You are not here,' he went in English. 'You are in wrong seat. Wrong wagon. Wrong country.'

Bit harsh I reckoned, just on account of September 1st 2001, Munich, 5–1 to England.

'Hold on up mate,' I goes, 'no need to distress yourself innit? Prepared to let bygones be bygones and that. You get another chance no doubting. Maybe when Michael Owen retires, hear what I'm saying?'

'See!' he turned round and said. 'The reservation it is for wagen 270. This is wagen 272. You are in wrong place.'

'Fair enough Franz,' I goes. 'Fair enough geezer. Still you got to turn round and say there ain't a lot of pressure on places round here am I right?' Half the seats were empty, fuck's sake. 'Seeing as I'm settled so cosy you let me carry on and have a little snooze or what? Stay mellow, know what I mean?'

'You move!' he went. 'Or I throw you off train!'

He really took that 5–1 to heart unfortunate.

'Franz,' I goes, 'you got to stay chilled mate. This ain't doing your old throbber no favours, you hear me? Course I move, seeing as what you want, always pleased to do a favour for a geezer innit? But you stay sweet eh? Think about your health pressures?'

He stood there while I got my bag.

'You got a buffet or what?' I went. 'I ain't half peckish I'm telling you. Even a bleeding tomato ketchup flavour bag of crisps liven me up a treat.'

'Wagen 270,' he turned round and said. 'You go.'

I went. Found my seat. Opposite some old biddy about eighty gave me the smile. Doing a spot of knitting and reading a magazine. German not Polish. Or Russian or Lithuanian. More to the point she got a pile of sandwiches on the table in front of her. Someone it paid to friend up.

'All right Helga?' I goes.

'Morgen,' she goes. Several times. Then she carried on chatting. Told me about their weather. Then the state of the country. Then her grandchildren. Then Borussia Dortmund. Least she may have done, I never had a fucking clue what she turned round and said. She went on in German so I went 'ja ja' when the time seemed right or nodded my bonce. She seemed like happy enough with that.

Hard to believe only it looked like she got cucumber sandwiches. I never ever gobbed a cucumber sandwich in my life. Or maybe it was some kind of gherkin they got out there. I started dribbling. Sleepier or hungrier, I was never sure which I was. It was either dozing or chasing the buffet or maybe headbutting the old lady and nicking her nosh.

Then Franz turned up again.

'Ah!' he went when he clocked me. 'You are here!' Fairly bleeding obvious you might turn round and say.

'All right Franz?'

'Ticket!'

'You already clocked my ticket.'

'Ticket!'

I gave him the fucking thing all over again.

'This is reservation.' He gave like an announcement.

'Fair enough.'

'This is platz reservation. Sitzplatz 52.'

'Correct.'

'I want ticket.'

'You got ticket.'

'This is platz reservation. Sitzplatz 52.'

'You turned round and said that Franz.'

'Where is ticket?'

'Jesus Christ Franz what more you want?' Mystery to me. I got all my tickets out, hundreds of the fuckers Noreen gave me or Elena gave me. He went through the lot.

'You have no ticket. Only seat reservation. You must pay me for ticket. Or I throw you off train.'

'Jesus mate, I ain't hardly going to get a seat reservation if I ain't got no bleedin' ticket, am I right? Got to be there somewhere or maybe they made a frigging screw up, left it out by mistake.'

'No mistake.'

'So how you reckon I got the reservation eh? Do me a favour you're doing my head in.'

'It is easy. For some people.' Meaning no doubting it was easy for some people like villains, criminals and English. I reckoned he was racially prejudiced.

Then just when things were turning nasty, next thing was pull out the sawnoffs, what came from opposite me was freeflow in a long dress.

Old biddy spoke English it turned out. Lot of it. She spoke it to our blood clot here.

'Excuse me Mr Inspector but it is obvious that this

gentleman must have a ticket. Do you really think he was able to buy a reservation without a ticket? There might be some people in Germany who know how to do this but not a foreigner, he would not be able to. Now he is a guest in our country and he comes from a friendly nation and there is nothing about him that suggests he is dishonest in any way. He looks like a clean and upright young man who has possibly mislaid his ticket or who was mistakenly not given one in the first place. I cannot believe that you can be such a terrible representative of our country and so inhospitable to our guests when we in Germany have such old traditions of harbouring the stranger. You should be ashamed!'

Old Franz never understood the half of what she was going on about. He only spoke the English he needed. Bit like me for that matter. She waved her knitting at him. Then she turned round and said it all again in German.

'I want ticket,' he went again. 'Or I throw you off train.' He learned that bit very well.

Then I picked up my Lithuanian phrasebook.

I spotted my ticket from Warsaw to Berlin. Been using it for a bookmark.

''Scuse me,' I went. 'Er, Franz. ''Scuse me, this what you looking for?'

He clocked it.

'Of course,' he went. Stamped it. Then he stamped on to their next passenger.

*

Me and Helga we eyeballed each other.

She started up giggling.

'Bit embarrassing,' I goes. 'Wound his clock I reckon. Bit unfortunate he was kind of correct.'

'Ach, no,' she went. 'He is a fascistic man. Of course he should have accepted your reservation. These people, they put on a uniform and they think they are the Gestapo.'

'Er, just a mo, Helga. Ain't it right we don't talk about them Gestapo these days? War was a long time ago and that? And the '66 World Cup? Best of mates now?'

'Some of us can talk about it, young man. I was in Berlin then. In 1945. I am allowed to talk about what I want.'

Jesus. I heard they got a spot of grief in Berlin.

'Jesus lady,' I goes. 'Reckon you got some serious aggravation then, am I right?'

'Yes, yes, I think you could call it quite serious aggravation.'

'Reckon my granddad he probably dropped some of them bombs on top of you.'

'I should think he did. Everyone else did. He was in the aeroplanes, your grandfather?'

'So my mum reckons. Could be telling porkies. Any of them bombs land on you?'

She gave me the gaze. Maybe wondering I was radio rental.

'Well, yes, they did land on me,' she went. 'Quite a lot

of things did actually. Tell me, young man, how did you know that my name was Helga?'

'Er . . . kind of a wild guess Helga. Kind of you looked like a Helga. Sort of straight and honest and beautiful and generous and—'

'There is no need to go over the top young man. My name is Helga Meinhof. I am very pleased to meet you. And you are?'

'Nicky Burkett. Out of Walthamstow. Meecha.'

'And you speak a little German then I understand?'

'Oh, er, kind of a few words like.' Kind of like fussball and goal and herr kapitan and Gestapo. Best to keep off that when I spent half an hour going ja ja to her like I was fluent. 'So where you learn your English then Helga or what? You ever been to Walthamstow?'

'I regret to say that I have not been to Walthamstow. I learned my English first at school. Then after the war I was a translator for the British forces. Then I married an English colonel. I was beautiful then.'

'Beautiful now Helga.'

'You are kind. We went back to England and lived in Camberley. Then he left me. I came back to Germany and became an actress and then a journalist and then I was the lover of the prime minister of Bavaria and then I became a member of our parliament and then I married and had three children and then I became a mountain climber. In recent times I have merely travelled. I have now been visiting friends in Warsaw and I am going back to Cologne where my house and my husband are. And you, Nicky? Where has your career led you?'

'Well, Helga, you could turn round and say I been out and about in the bargain. Wandsworth, Ford, Hollesley Bay up Suffolk, Dover, Brixton, all where my career led me. Then I retired though. Took up with Noreen my bird. I stays mostly in Walthamstow now except I just went to Lithuania.'

'Lithuania. That must have been very interesting. Both historically and culturally it is a fascinating place.'

'Hear what you're saying mate. Unfortunate though I got to leg it out of there before I got too much of all that. Still.'

'Do I understand from this that you experienced some problems there?'

'Few problems yeah Helga. Fact, fell in with some serious attitude problems. Major confusions. Make it all worse, I so trussed up now I can't never even take my clothes off before I get home I'm telling you.' It was all coming out. All my problems.

'Excuse me? Have you suffered a serious injury? It is very intimate?'

'Nah. Bleeding fortunate I ain't though on that account. Nah, problem a bit different from that. See I got paper all over my body.'

'Paper?' She was clocking me kind of curious.

'Notes. Dosh. Buckets of wedge.'

'Money?'

'Yeah Helga. Wedge. Packs of folding. All a bit tricky. Just now I got paper in every pocket.'

'I think you must tell me about this Nicky.' Her little beadies got a right twinkle in them. 'Am I correct in thinking that there is something illegal in this?'

I was taking a bit of a shine to old Helga. Kind of a homeboy. When she reckoned there was a touch of the illegals she showed up right perky.

'Well illegal got to be going too far,' I turned round and said. 'Least I ain't got a fucking starter whether it was illegal. Illegal them trying to bop me I reckon. What I done thought I ain't decided on my plea yet. Know what I mean?'

'I think so.' She was waiting.

I was fucking starving. I never could talk any more till I got some nosh in my belly. I was rolexed.

'Would you like a sandwich Nicky?' she went.

'They cucumber?' Hoping it got to be anything, Japanese seaweed, Norwegian hamster, not cucumber.

'They are cucumber, yes.'

'My favourite.'

She passed them across. I swallowed half of them straight off. Left her the other half generous. She gave me coffee out of her flask. I was happy as a rat in a sewer.

'Now I think you should tell me your story,' she goes.

'All kind of confidential,' I goes. 'All kind of lawyers only type of thing.'

'I think you should tell me anyway, don't you?'

So I did.

TWENTY-SIX

FAR AS I COULD clock it, this was how it went down.

Jonas was a villain in Lithuania. Got a good position there, geezer with a pukka rep, but opportunities grew limited there so he decided to take his trade elsewhere.

Professional openings beckoned from Blighty. He came to Edmonton where he reckoned the streets were paved.

First off everything was hunky. Jonas was able to employ his skills. He made a good wodge of dosh and he got his bredren by his side.

Unfortunate then things went arsewise. Business dropped. More hours less pay. Red tape. Probably the Common Market.

Then all the gangsters came from Russia and wanted a piece. Doing a runner or just expanding, one or the other. And there was another complication. Lithuanians and all the rest in North London were tired of getting zapped. Started to fight back.

So a way of life was dying out. Jonas was getting thin. Then would you believe he got touched by a feeler. Feeler in blue. So because of the situation he got to weigh it up. He considered the odds. He took the Old Bill sixpence.

Old Bill as usual failed to protect their grasses, any fucker tell him that, and he got whacked.

Some reason though Old Bill got a smacking in the bargain. This one still a puzzler to me. Why it was they punished the DI from Chingford? Went for him special, no doubting.

Then the Yard came in, never identified only they looked like National Crime Squad. They wanted my money back off me only Noreen sent me up Lithuania. They pulling the plug on some wheeling? The DI was bent and they found out?

Next, Elena and me we collected Jonas's dosh from the post office. Some of it was maybe off Old Bill, the rest from his bits of work. And several geezers reckoned they were owed a percentage.

Elena's gaff got surveillance. So the Lithuanians in London were tight with the Lithuanians in Lithuania. Maybe same people. And they were looking for whatever we got to hide.

Elena gave me a tenper. Then she did the seductivity. Made her play. And all that. Mine not to reason.

We legged it. We left on the chuffer where I got ambushed. Least glad to say it was my neighbour got ambushed.

They never tried for the dosh though. Not off me. Maybe reckoned it was on Elena? Or never knew what they were after?

Or Elena was with them? Nah. Made no sense for giving me the dosh then trying to take it back. Which they never.

Although maybe I served my purpose with Elena, protection for her till we got on the Germany train.

Then where it was she went? No fucking idea. Still in Poland or more likely going up Germany some other way.

'Jesus H. Christ!' I went sudden.

'What is it Nicky?'

'You reckon maybe the Yard got there before? That razor in her cupboard was off some Yardie inspector? Or she belled them after we made the cash? They went how she could keep the rest while they got the Firm's money back off me? Bit of a tempter, am I right? See where I'm headed? See my road?'

'I think I can see your road Nicky, stretching into the distance, then I can see a bridge over a river, then the road on the other side leading to a fairy princess.'

'No need to get carried away Helga.'

'I am sorry. But it is exciting.'

'So where you reckon that DI from Chingford fits in that got a smacking?'

'Well, Nicky, first I think there is no romantic connection between Elena and Old Bill.'

'Nah?'

'No. I do not think Elena is the type to have the razor of Bill the police inspector in her cupboard. I think it is more likely that the razor came from another liaison. Or perhaps there is a purely innocent explanation.'

'Innocent?'

'But it does seem possible that she gave the police's money to you. Perhaps she thought that they would not come after her if she did this.'

'So you reckon it was Old Bill tried to whack me? Jesus.'

'No. I don't think so. It seems that it was Lithuanians on the train and that they were only trying to kill you. They did not search the body for money.'

'True words Helga.'

Helga was giving me good sympathy. Like a counsellor. Only more use.

'As you say, Elena saw you as her protector until she reached Germany. They probably saw you as the same.'

'Kind of a hard man?'

'And when they had killed you they could take from her whatever she had. They may not know she had money in the bag, only that something came from England.'

'Drugs?'

'Yes.'

'Sweet.'

'But I think you may still have a problem when you return to England, don't you?'

'Who me?'

'I think you may be right when you think that the English police will be involved. There is no proof but it is significant that they attacked before they even knew what Elena had received. When you arrived in Vilnius Elena was already being watched. Did she say how long they had been watching her?'

'Nah.'

'I suspect it was only a couple of days. Yet someone knew how to find her. But they had not done so before now. I think that Lithuanians came from London but that police also came, or at least were in touch with police in Lithuania. They found Jonas's friends. His family. They found Elena and told someone to watch her. Then I expect they watched the gangsters who were watching her.'

'Jesus Helga. How you know all this?'

'Oh . . .' she went vague. 'I have also been followed in my time. It was some time ago . . .'

'Jesus Helga.'

But she was never giving out more.

'So you reckon,' I carried on, 'them Old Bill are with them ones wanting to give me the big snooze? Fuck.'

'How otherwise would they act so fast? But I think it is police who are trying to cover something up. I think it is maybe the first one. The man who gave you the money.'

Finlay. Last seen in the gutter with a dent in his bonce.

'He in bad shape Helga. Got a bad headache.'

'His friends.'

TT? After all this time we known each other, that shitface TT?

Shit.

Then another point.

'Helga,' I went. 'You reckon they still clocking me?'

'Yes. I do.'

'You reckon they lift me some place?'

'Yes. Perhaps in England. But if you try to run off, before then.'

'Jesus Helga.'

We had a pause.

'Would you like another sandwich?'

'Nah, I'm right Helga.'

'Or a cake?' Their trolley was just passing.

'Yeah. Here, hold on up Helga, I got plenty of dosh.'

'Please do not take any of your money out of your pockets. I will buy a cake and some more coffee for you.'

She did.

I gave it thinking. When the trolley wallah passed on I turned round and spoke.

'Helga,' I went. 'You want to look after my spends for me or what?'

She stirred.

'Are you sure, Nicky?' she went.

'Yeah.'

'Are you a good judge of character?'

'Nah. Me, I'm a shit judge of character. I made most of the worst choices a geezer ever made. You straight?'

'Yes I am straight.'

'You reckon it's kosher?'

More pause.

'Yes, I think it is best.'

'You want a tenper? Bit of a drink?'

'Excuse me?'

'You reckon on an agent fee?'

'Certainly not. I would be insulted.'

'Give you a holiday in Walthamstow. Fact pay for it myself. Longest street market in Europe. Dog track. Top curry area.'

'I am very grateful.'

'So why you do this Helga?'

'To see justice done. Because you are a nice polite young man. For the excitement. Because I do not like the police.'

Every one of them a puzzler.

I never got a lot of options though. Least, considering she was right I never got a lot of options. Considering she was wrong, I could sail straight home.

'Helga,' I turned round and said. 'I still got a problem round that DI. Why you reckon they whacked him, them Lithuanians in London?'

'I do not know. There was something between them. Perhaps he was Jonas's controller. Perhaps they thought they could stop the investigations if they killed him. On the other hand, perhaps he was involved with both sides.'

'Like you turned round and said. Him or his mates gave the words on me going up Lithuania.'

'They wanted your money back when the other police became involved. They wanted Jonas's money back.'

'Dosh,' I goes philosophical. 'Root of all evil Helga.'

I ate my cake. We drank our coffees.

Then I gave thinking on the practicals. Some difficulties.

'Helga,' I goes, 'how you reckon we transfer all this paper over from me to you and no fucker clocks it?'

'I do not know Nicky.'

Then she started cackling. Me in the bargain. We both reckoned the same thing. Cause a bit of a stir going off up the toilets together. I was all for a bit of equality, different ages and that. All the same there could be people reckon something kind of suspicious, Helga and me going in there careless. They might be reckoning we maybe never went in there for a touch of the other like most birds and geezers. Even they did, it could draw attention we never wanted.

I clocked around the carriage. The way I saw it every

one of the passengers looked like rozzers' narks. Not do the exchange there. Get lifted in four minutes.

We gave it brain. Least she did.

Then she went out loud.

'I have got it. Nicky I know what to do.'

'Yeah?'

'We will exchange our clothes.'

'Jesus Helga!'

TWENTY-SEVEN

I RECKONED SHE WAS maybe a crossie.

Maybe she reckoned I was a crossie.

'Jesus Helga I ain't wearing no cardigan!'

'Not at all Nicky, not at all. I was considering only our undergarments.'

'Jesus Helga! You making it worse here!'

'You told me that you had many pockets in your clothes. So have I. I even have an undervest that has a pocket in it. Do you have something similar which I could wear?'

'Nah! No vests! And Helga I ain't wearing your knickers!'

She cackled fit to bust a garter. Most fun she had since the bombs fell. 'No,' she went, 'I do not mean that we should exchange our most intimate garments. When I said undergarments I meant to say those clothes which were not on top. Perhaps shirts if they have pockets. I can put money in my under vest but we do not need to exchange . . . I notice that you are wearing two pairs of trousers, yes?'

'Yeah . . .' I looked down. Forgot I still got two pairs of strides on, left from Lithuania. As it goes I was hot now.

'Then you could take off one pair which will have money in it. I could put them on under mine. I think they will fit me because I am more slim than many women. Also as for the length, I think you are a bit, how do you say . . . ?'

'Bit of a short arse.'

'Bit of a short arse, exactly. I think we should try it, do you agree?' She was that excited I was worried she might do herself a mischief. She was giggling like a French tickler.

'All right Helga. All right mate. Do whatever you fancy, you got me? Except them undergarments, know what I mean?'

She got it sorted. She went out first for a recce. Went in the toilet, checked no-one followed her up there, came out, went up the buffet, came back. Far as we could tell it was all clean. She reckoned on where I could leave the clobber in a corner in the toilet for when she came in behind.

Soon I went up there. Took a good butcher's on the way and Helga following behind took a good butcher's. I went in their toilet and she stood outside, next customer. Just so long as no fucker came up with the screaming trots or some bleeding baby and reckoned they got right of way. I took one pair of jeans off and my shirt. Already they were full of dosh, still I packed all the notes there from my jacket. Left the jeans and shirt in the corner, put the jacket back on and buggered off out. Helga went in. I never stayed, look like some perve standing outside. I went back to our seats. When she came back she looked kind of bigger about the bust and the hips but I hoped no fucker noticed.

Back I goes. Some bastard went in the toilet in between. When he came out, big butch Polish geezer he was never tempted by her blouse she left in the corner. I went in, took my jacket off, put her blouse on. Shoulders were tight, heard a bit of ripping. I put the jacket on again, covered it up nicely.

Then I took the jacket off again and clocked the mirror.

Jesus H. Christ. Helga was never the frilly type and her blouse was more Madonna than Britney Spears. All the same we knew what it was.

Fucking girl's blouse.

I kept my jacket on the rest of the journey. Well buttoned.

Not long after that we got up Berlin.

We turned round and said our goodbyes, me and Helga. Both going on to Cologne only we reckoned separate was

241

best. We gave over our addresses and numbers. She wrote hers down. I remembered it then chucked it. She reckoned she'd be in touch. I fucking hoped so.

Course, maybe there was no fucker on our train watching us at all. Helga was in with the Bill. Or she was an A-level con artist.

She went off waddling a bit in my jeans packed with paper. I got me a slice of pizza and climbed on the next train.

I was going home. For definite now. Thank fuck for that.

TWENTY-EIGHT

Eurostar came up Waterloo.

On Eurostar they spoke English. Up Waterloo they spoke English. I was like a pig in shit. On the chuffer I got a cup of rosie. All I needed now was a trip down the market and a pint up the Chequers and I was barking.

'Excuse me sir.'

'All right mate?'

'Excuse me sir, could you come this way a moment?'

'Eh?'

'Nicholas Burkett?'

'Who wants to know?'

'Let me show you my ID. Customs and Excise.'

'I just been through Customs innit?'

'We would just like to have a word, Mr Burkett. Purely a routine matter.'

Four of them. Purely fucking routine.

'See all your IDs mate.'

'We are only obliged to show you one.'

'See all your IDs or I ain't coming.'

Not much I could do but they showed them. One was from the Met as expected. Not C and E. More like the silent partner.

'Could you just step in here please.'

I went. In a room. Looked like a normal office. Except it got the glass panel. Never pick your nose unless you want it on video.

'Could I see your passport please?'

I gave it over.

'Could we look in your bag sir please?'

'All yours mate.'

'Could you open it for us?'

'Nah.'

'What?'

'Nah.'

Put them in a tizz. Everyone always opened their bags. No reason otherwise. Except my reason. Fuck 'em.

'Mr Burkett, if you will not open your bag yourself we may have to detain you while we involve bomb disposal experts. You may be here for a long time.'

'Suit yourself mate. I ain't in a rush.'

'Why will you not open your bag?'

'Ain't in the mood.'

'Mr Burkett, you are not being at all co-operative.'

'Reckon.'

Pause. Clocked each other. Then tried for something else to do until some geezer made a decision on the bag.

'Mr Burkett we will now give you a non-intimate body search.'

No comment.

'Please would you take off your jacket then raise your hands and place your legs apart.'

In my time I had all the body searches. Intimate, non-intimate, half way fucking intimate you name it. I co-operated.

Even though I was wearing a bird's blouse.

I stared them down. Like it was no problem only what every geezer wore on Eurostar. They all clocked me, waiting for the explanation. Never came.

'How long have you been abroad Mr Burkett?'

One moment I reckoned he meant a broad.

'Few days.'

'Business or pleasure?'

'Pleasure.' I had to cackle. Main pleasure was getting home.

'Why are you laughing?'

'Who me?'

'Where have you been on this trip?'

'Lithuania.'

'For what purpose?'

'Pleasure.'

'What kind of pleasure?'

'None of your business mate.'

'Have you brought anything back with you? Alcohol, tobacco?'

'Bottle of vodka. Box of chocolates.'

'Where are they?'

'In my bag.'

'Will you open it?'

'Nah.'

'Why are you wearing that blouse?'

'Who me?'

'That's who I'm talking to. Why are you wearing that blouse?'

'What blouse?'

'That blouse you are wearing. Why are you wearing that blouse?'

'Dunno mate. Picked it up on the train.'

'You picked it up on the train.'

'What I turned round and said.'

'Why did you pick it up on the train?'

'Dunno mate.'

'You don't know why you picked it up?'

'Nah.'

'It's a woman's blouse.'

'Nah!'

Then the Met man spoke.

'SHUT IT!'

Pause.

'Who me?'

'Shut the whole fucking lot of you up!'

'This being recorded I hope?' I went. 'Remember I got to sign the record of all interviews.'

'I'll sign your fucking mush in a minute my friend.'

I stayed stum. Customs never beat anyone up that I heard of. Old Bill did.

He came over and he tore the zip on my bag open. Then they all stood waiting. But none of us got blew up.

He put my bag on their table and he went through it. Then he went through it again. Then a C and E geezer got a metal detector. Then they called a dog in for sniffing. The bag and me. Then they went through everything again.

Fuck all.

I got to account for my dosh. No problem. Even offered them a bribe, few thousand Belarussian roubles. Very fucking funny. Wanted to clock my tickets. No problem. Seemed like they never knew how I cut short my holiday from my original. They could find out. If they checked.

I was there about an hour. Like old times. Told them fuck all. Then they got to let me go.

*

I belled Noreen on her mobile. Middle of the night but she likely got the mobile by the bed.

'Yeah?' she went sleepy.

'Noreen, I interrupting anything? You got a few geezers there and that?'

Bit of silence.

'Nicky?'

'Who you think doll?'

'Nicky!'

'Yeah babe!'

'Don't you babe me Nicky!' Only she was laughing laughing. 'Nor doll me you wicked boy. Nicky where are you?'

'Waterloo station. Going to get a cab.'

'Waterloo? Nicky you're supposed to be in Lithuania!'

'Long story girl. I come by you?'

'Yeah!'

Brilliant bird Noreen. Bleeding brilliant girl. Best a geezer could get.

'On my way Noreen. Soon as I get a cab, right?'

'Yeah.'

Cabbies were outside the station. Quiet time. I went up the head of the line. Geezer keen for business as always.

'All right geezer?' I went.

'Uh.'

'You keen on Old Bill?'

'Uh?'

'You lose them, case they're trailing?'

'Must be fucking joking.'

'Fair enough John. Still we best be going.' I got in.

'Anywhere particular or you just want to fucking drive round all night?'

'Walthamstow.'

'Jesus.' Only time they liked going up Walthamstow was when they were on their way home up Gants Hill where all the cabbies came from. He started off like facing a prison sentence.

I took a butcher's through the back window. Maybe getting followed maybe not. Anyhow they got the technology these days. On my plates I could lose them soon enough but not in a motor. And I got nothing to hide so I remembered. We went home.

She was waiting by the window. Came running down the stairs even though I got my key.

Flung her arms round me. And legs. Held on tight.

'Noreen you little darlin'!'

'Mmm mmm mmm Nicky!' She kissed me eleven times in ten seconds.

(She was a bleeding brilliant bird Noreen.)

'Nicky you come upstairs and you tell me exactly all about everything you hear?'

'Right girl.' We went up. She kept touching me all the way up the stairs. We got up there eventual and I put my bag down and took my jacket off.

'Nicky what in hell you got on? Looks like some old lady's blouse or what!'

I cackled.

'Noreen I got a very great lot to tell you.'

'That some old lady's blouse Nicky for real?'

'Yeah it some old lady's blouse Noreen.'

She got the tea going.

'I got a lot to tell,' I went again. While she made the rosie we touched and we nuzzled. Then while we sat there I told her the lot.

Well nearly.

TWENTY-NINE

I BELLED RAMEEZ next morning after he woke up lunchtime.

I belled him swift on account of if I omitted to bell him then he heard the story off some other geezer and he reckoned I might be owing him he was likely for being very displeased.

Rameez got displeased with you generally involved you missing a bit of your fifth gear.

Good job we were mates really. I got a bit of leverage on account of how he reckoned my sister was the best piece of goods in Walthamstow.

So I belled him soon as he woke up at eleven then we

met up Shere Khan's curry house on Hoe St for breakfast. Me, I got a few pakoras and a cup of tea, kind of a snack. Rameez when he breakfasted out he liked to keep regular like at home. So they gave him sugar puffs and four cups of tea, special customer.

'Morning Rameez.'

'Morning Nicky Burkett.'

'Morning Aftab.'

'Morning Nicky.'

'Morning Afzal.'

'Morning Nicky.'

Javed was off collecting some early dues.

They brought us our grub. We sat by the window. Outside on Hoe St Rameez's Audi was stood standing on their yellow lines. Moons and stars all over, every sensible geezer in Walthamstow knew it was Rameez's.

Except would you believe fucking Sureways parking. Or maybe they just got excited clocking a real ticket instead of one they made up. Two of their fuckers stood by it pulling out their papers.

I started giggling.

Rameez got a glazed look on his boat.

'Aftab,' he went.

'Rameez.'

'I am a peace-loving geezer.'

'Rameez.'

'But everyone got to show some respect, am I right?'

'You are right Rameez. Spot on.'

'Now you be telling them fuckers out there the right words, yeah?'

'Rameez.'

Aftab goes out the eater and he stands by the geezers quiet. Then he pulls out a sword. He got it down his trouser leg, got to be very uncomfortable and maybe dangerous. He lays his sword on the Audi.

Then he had the right words.

Geezers apologised. Tore up their papers and went away.

Aftab comes back.

'Now where were we?' goes Rameez.

'Rameez I be reckoning on bringing you up to date.'

'Nicky I heard how you been out the borough and then came back again in a taxi this morning.'

'Correct Rameez.'

'Maybe you is coming back hasty because you remembered how you ain't yet given me my twenty per from your drink off the DI, you hear what I'm saying?'

I pulled out my wad.

'You want it in roubles Rameez?'

'Very amusing Nicky.'

'Rameez I never got the oppo before. Never clocked you like before I got to make an exit.'

'How much you reckon twenty per to be?' he went.

'Never my strong point Rameez. Only I had a count up

in my gaff. How I reckon it, twenty per of one hundred is twenty. Twenty per of two hundred got to be forty. So twenty per of three hundred got to be sixty. I carries on like this and I reckons twenty per of three big ones got to be six hundred. You with me?'

'Nicky you remember I got A-level Maths?'

'Remember Rameez. Stayed on in the sixth form for it. How I heard it, you reckoned it was useful for your chosen career.'

'Exact same Nicky. And you be pleased to know that six moderates is correct.'

I counted it out. Gave it over. He nodded and put it in his jacket.

'Could be several more yet Rameez. Part of the same picture.'

'Hoping so Nicky. Six moderates ain't very fucking big pickings, know what I mean?'

'Hear what you're saying Rameez. Only problem we got just now though, I got the readies in potential but I ain't got the readies just exactly to hand, you get me?'

Rameez took a spoonful of sugar puffs. Sip of rosie. He clocked me over his spoon.

'Nicky,' he went, 'you telling me we got a liquidity problem here?'

The fuck he talking about, liquidity? One moment I reckoned he got something in his spoon.

'Rameez,' I went, 'I reckon I best tell you the knockings,

start to finish.'

'I reckon you best had Nicky.'

I gave it to him, what he did know and what he never knew. Rameez he got A-level Maths, only in the bargain he got A-level first class lie detecting. Just on account of he liked to slice geezers never meant he was missing in the spot the shit department.

It was all kind of confusing in the calculations though. Reckoning the dosh came through from Helga Rameez was due his twenty per. Part of the same enterprise. Reckoning she kept it for herself or she got struck by lightning, Rameez was still due only he never got it.

I never fancied a trip to Cologne with Rameez for beating up an old lady.

One other point, I never knew how much it was. Left it for Helga to count up.

So I told it. When I finished talking they were so gobsmacked Aftab spoke out of turn.

'You doshed the paper . . .'

'Some old German bird . . .' went Afzal.

'Never counted it . . .' went Rameez. 'On account of you reckoned she got to be pukka, some old German bird you met on a passenger train between one place and another place.'

'Warsaw and Berlin,' I goes helpful.

They stared. Fact everyone in the eater stared. Staff stopped serving.

'But you get your twenty per Rameez,' I goes. 'Whatever much it is.'

'Nicky Burkett . . .' he went.

'If it comes.'

They stared. Total silence maybe one minute.

Then my mobile rang.

It was TT. DS TT Holdsworth, Chingford's finest.

'Nicky,' he went.

'Nicky Burkett don't want to fucking talk to you,' I goes. 'Leave a fucking message.'

'Nicky we need you up the nick at four. Heard you were back. Welcome.'

I clocked the mobile. Got to be they traced me.

'Nicky Burkett don't want to fucking talk to you,' I went.

'Nicky we got Lithuanians coming at four.'

Never even worth answering.

'We need you there for identification.'

'What?'

'We pulled him in on a motoring charge.'

'Who?'

'One of them Lithuanians up Edmonton. Gave him a producer.'

'I ain't going up Edmonton nick.'

'We told him to produce his documents at Walthamstow today. At four.'

'Producer you go up your local nick.'

'I know that Nicky. But he don't know that. And we charged him with careless driving as well.'

'Jesus that should frighten him TT. Likely bottle off out the country. The fuck makes you reckon he turns up?'

'We know where he lives. He bought a fucking house Nicky. His home.'

'Bought a gaff? A gangster?'

'Trying to go legit. Assets. Liquidity.'

More of that liquidity.

'So we get him down, you identify him then we charge him with murder.'

Something not very kosher going down here.

'And if I never come?'

'We pick you up at three.'

'And if I never identify him?'

'You best identify him.'

Something very very not kosher.

'Check you later TT.' I switched off.

I stared at my mobile. I was never very happy. I was being set up for something. So was the Lithuanian geezer.

Convenient us being in the same place the same time.

I told Rameez and his boys.

'Walthamstow?' they went. 'Charging up Walthamstow nick? On motoring where they don't charge you up the nick and on murder where they smack you good? It gotta be up Chingford or nowhere man. Very very fishy.'

'Nicky you got to make a call,' goes Rameez.

'You be there supporting?'

'Course. Ready and waiting. But you got to make a call first.'

'Who?'

'Someone.'

'Gotcha.'

I used his phone not mine. I belled George my old warrant officer.

Only Old Bill I ever trusted was George. Always round our gaff he was when I was a villain. Never paid my fines, George came seven in the morning, got a spot of breakfast, took me up the cells. Generally came on his pushbike so we got to walk back up there. One time we even went on the bus, least I went on the bus so George rode pedalling behind. Every time I got sent down George got my fines quashed, even only a week inside. He was like part of the family.

George was kind of a bitter geezer now though. His old job he worked up the courts, did the warrants, then the cells or sat in court. Nothing he didn't know. Then they got privatised. They gave George a choice, go back on the beat or work civilian. Last thing George ever wanted was go back on the beat, fucking shifts again, so he went civilian. Never the same geezer. They whacked his wages. Whacked his pension. He still used the Met social club up Chigwell only he felt like he was never entitled. He was one bitter geezer.

But he was a straight goer was George.

I got him up his office.

'George,' I goes.

'Nicky Burkett, bugger me,' he went. 'You ain't in trouble again Nicky I hope?'

'George where are you this minute?'

'You know where I am Nicky, you just rang me here. In my office up the courts.'

'So you are George. So I did. George, I needs you. Immediate.'

'Immediate?'

'Immediate George. Five minutes you can do it. You make Shere Khan's on Hoe St? We got very very big aggravation this afternoon in Walthamstow. I needs an honest copper.'

'Jesus Nicky I ain't a copper now at all you know that.'

'You got the leads George. Please. And don't breathe.'

I never ever went please to George.

He was there in six minutes.

THIRTY

Four o'clock and I was sitting drinking tea in reception at Walthamstow nick.

'He ain't coming,' I turned round and said.

'We don't know that,' went TT. 'Be here if he ain't got his brains addled. Not worth having a warrant out for a careless driving. He'll want to get it cleared up.'

I wanted to ask TT what he knew. What he reckoned was going down. If he was involved. Or if he was only a stiff for them.

I kept stum.

'What you want me to do?' I went. 'Yell out fuck me it's that murderer? Even if I never clocked him before?'

I was wired. They never searched me being a witness.

'Give us the sign. See what he does. First we see what he says about the careless driving.'

'Thought you got a summons on a Careless, straight up the court?'

'True. But he don't know that.'

They were wanting him to do something. And TT was nervous. He was fingering his moustache. Except he never got one. He was sweating.

In reception they got three other Old Bill. Out the back I got the feeling they got plenty, only I came in the front with them. They never wanted me to clock what they got out the back.

Reception was busy as normal.

At the desk was a woman lost her dog.

Next was a Care in the Community. Not sure what he came in for, maybe get warm after he been down Casualty and in the library.

Next was a producer. Genuine producer. Produce his documents after he got stopped in his motor. Course he was young and black. Nothing better to do, Old Bill stop a few black geezers.

Behind him was Jimmy Foley.

They discharged Jimmy the day before, reckoned they needed the bed for someone more dead than he was. I belled him earlier, let him know the SP. Spite of his injuries he was down there like dysentery. Limping and hopping and gasping he came in there beaming. Reckoned he was bound to be on bail for something or other with conditions of reporting to police so he was there legit. TT was fucking leery when he clocked Jimmy. Not part of their plan. Whatever the fuck their plan was. Jimmy told him he was wanting for being a witness in the bargain while he was there. Very clear Old Bill never wanted him anywhere near.

Two doors they got in their copshop between the outside and the desk. Supposed to wait after the middle one, never interfere in private business gassing up the counter.

It crashed open. Whack.

'You fuckin' fuckers! You fuckin' bastard fuckin' fuckers!'

Not a Lithuanian. It was Manky Mackay, Tennents drinker, usually outside the post office on the market.

His plates never touched the ground. They fucked him right off out the back, let him cool down somewhere. No interruptions please.

'Not very Lithuanian,' I went.

'Shut it Nicky.'

We waited. We sipped.

Door opened again. Tall dark stocky geezer. Bags under his mincers.

It was a Lithuanian.

It was never the geezer stabbed Jonas though. He was short and thin and ginger.

But it was the geezer tried to stab me on the train.

Fuck me.

He got someone with him, maybe an interpreter. And another one. Two interpreters. And they got a motor parked outside on the yellow line. Driver still in there. Three interpreters. I never recognised any of them.

Old Bill cleared all the other punters out right quick. Jimmy they bypassed.

Lithuanian geezer came up the desk. With his papers. And his mates.

'Ah yes,' went the desk man. 'What have we got here?'

Geezer pushed the papers over. 'Not guilty,' he went. Learned it. Unfortunate I burst out laughing.

'You ain't been charged yet,' went the desk man. 'You've got to plead up the court mate. Let's have a look at these papers shall we? Ah yes. You are, er, Antanas, er, Maksim . . . Maksimaitis?'

Then I clocked two things.

First was DI Finlay looking through the window in the door to the back.

So he got out the hospital in the bargain. Sudden it got me thinking. Was he in charge of this? Or the geezer from the Yard? Or National Crime Squad? What the fuck?

Second I clocked the Lithuanian geezer. Clocking me.

One moment he was trying to remember. Went vague.

Then it came.

He went up very sharp. Gave me the stare. Eyes wide.

Then he went something hurried in Lithuanian.

Then all their heads went up. Looking hard round the room. Smelling for what they knew. And Old Bill knew. Everyone knew now. This was it.

We waited. Then they moved.

Shooters.

Fuck me. Lithuanians got them, brought them out from inside their coats. Not just stickers now but shooters. Sawnoffs. Old-fashioned sawnoffs, so they learned some English habits.

I was on the floor.

Then hell broke out.

Geezers in combat burst from the back. And padded vests. And police rifles. But the Lithuanians were gone. Out the door. Piled in their motor.

I got up and looked out the window. More Old Bill went out the back of the station, into Greenleaf Rd and down on to Forest Rd. Some of them armed.

Then would you believe a different lot were coming up Forest Rd from Blackhorse. All wearing sniper jackets and caps. These were never Walthamstow nor even Finlay's squad. These were very serious attitude geezers.

'Lay down your arms!' they yelled out very loud.

Then I realised something was wrong.

They were never yelling it to the Lithuanians. They were yelling it to the other Old Bill.

Only the Lithuanians never knew this. All they knew was someone was yelling at them.

Then it started.

I ran up the door for clocking the whole action. But lay down.

Lithuanians fired at the serious geezers on Forest Rd. About twenty Old Bill, crouching while they moved. None of them hit. They kept coming. Held their fire.

Old Bill off Greenleaf Rd never. They shot. They were shooting at Lithuanians. Motor was starting off, one of them still hanging out the side, he got hit and dropped.

I slid back in the nick. None of that thank you.

'All right Bridget?' I went.

The woman reporting her lost mutt was Bridget Tansley off the *Walthamstow Guardian*. I belled her before and she got down there. I wanted a witness and now I wanted Old Bill to know I got a witness, case they got any ideas about taking me out.

'Hello Nicky,' she went loud. 'Excuse me officers I am Bridget Tansley from the *Guardian*. Can I have a few quotes please on the present situation?'

'Get the fuck down!' went someone from behind the desk. One quote anyhow.

She did. She lay down beside me looking out the door when we could. Only time I ever got Bridget lying down by me.

Everything was whizzing. Old Bill whizzing in all

directions. Bullets fucking whizzing in the windows and walls now. Me feeling like I was whizzing. It was madness.

Lithuanians went the only way they could. Left their mate wounded or croaking, flew out in their motor the other way up Forest Rd toward the Town Hall.

They never got half way. Back windows got shot out, tyres got shot out. Motor went up the pavement and in one of the houses. Geezers piled out and ran.

They ran into Lloyd Park. Disturb the ducks. Behind the trees they were shooting back now. Shooting at anyone. They got two lots to choose. Up one side of Forest Rd they got the Old Bill who came off Greenleaf Rd. I reckoned they were Finlay's, maybe the other DI except I was never sure which way he folded. Bill went in and out the shops, the radio shop, Sedgwicks sports shop, the Sally Army, poking out their shooters and firing. Other side of Forest Rd they got the new Old Bill with their caps and armbands. Somehow George got them activated, whoever they were. They went in the houses and the mini front gardens, only they were lagging on account of they got no real shelter. Lithuanians were shooting in their direction but they never returned it, not waste their bullets when they couldn't clock them. They only got one lot of targets they could see.

Old Bill were shooting each other.

Fuck I was enjoying this.

Only problem was the Lithuanians might still get away up the Bell Corner before the Town Hall.

Then Rameez and his boys arrived.

Never too sure whose side they were on or what the fuck they were even doing there. All the same they saw a gap and they filled it, good business principles. Geezers likely for escaping up Forest Rd past the Bell so they blocked Forest Rd before the Bell. Never had shooters so they got to find some other way. They stopped the motors. Got the drivers out. Overturned the motors. Siphoned the petrol. Brought their bottles with them. Started throwing bombs. No special targets, not even any special direction only started throwing them about and making a fucking din.

Which it did.

Lithuanians clocked that and they had to go sideways.

They went in the William Morris museum.

Walthamstow got its share of museums. Some geezer reckoned Walthamstow got nothing you wanted to remember. Other geezers felt different. Proving it they got museums. They got them in The Village and then they got William Morris.

They took us round his museum on a school trip. While we were there I wrote down one of his quotes: 'If I were to work ten hours a day at work I despised and hated I should spend my leisure in drinking.'

Geezer got a lot going for him.

I came down Forest Rd now with Bridget behind Old Bill. No sign of Jimmy Foley, seemed he stayed by the cop shop.

Crashes came from the museum. Glass. Jesus, they were smashing the windows so they could shoot out. It was like the westerns. Only three Lithuanians and about forty police only it seemed like an even battle now. Specially as Old Bill were shooting each other.

They were still passing up both sides of Forest Rd. Two or three from Finlay's crew went down. Difficult to know who shot them but they were shot.

Now they were in position for an assault on the front of the museum. Lying down flat firing. Behind the posts firing. Then turning round firing at the other Old Bill.

Too good to last. Some time they got to realise something wrong here.

I hoped all the shooting was never damaging old William's fabrics and that in his museum. Tiles and carpets and paintings and all kinds of whatnots he got in there.

Bridget taking photos and yacking into her tape like it was all her birthdays in one.

Then their loudspeaker started up again, New Bill from Blackhorse. Just when it was getting interesting they made another attempt for stopping it all.

'THIS IS AN ANNOUNCEMENT TO ALL THOSE POLICE OFFICERS IN FRONT OF THE WILLIAM MORRIS MUSEUM. THIS IS CHIEF SUPERINTENDENT BRADLEY OF THE METROPOLITAN POLICE. LAY DOWN YOUR ARMS. DO NOT PROCEED WITH THIS OPERATION. I REPEAT, LAY DOWN YOUR ARMS.

YOU ARE INSTRUCTED TO HALT THIS ACTION. WITHDRAW FROM YOUR POSITIONS AND SUBMIT YOURSELVES TO MY AUTHORITY.'

Bit of a pause after that.

Then another crash from William Morris.

Not the front windows. They got to be going out the back. Escaping. Past the bowling green and the playgrounds and the duckponds.

Finlay and a few broke cover. Ignored this Bradley. Ran up the front entrance of the museum. Stormed in shooting.

No answer. It went quiet.

The rest came back. Bradley's boys went up to them and arrested them. Jesus Christ. It was New Bill arresting Old Bill. Got the cuffs out. Hoped they used the fucking new-style ones near as chopped your hands off. Led them away. Got a squad of vans behind. Special riot vans, mean-looking.

Bridget was going mental, scribbling and chattering like a parrot on speed. And she got the mobile going now in the bargain.

Then it all went very quiet indeed. No traffic on Forest Rd. No birds singing neither.

Then Finlay came out the museum. Bradley moved up and arrested him personal. Led him away.

Choppers arrived. Ambulances. Hundreds more uniforms. Barriers went up. News blackout, no-one inside.

Except Bridget and me we were already inside.

*

We walked up William Morris pleased as you like. In the door, let it slam behind us.

'Mind the fucking stained glass! Only mind the fucking stained glass!'

It was Bertie the caretaker. He was hiding under his desk opposite the entrance. Hallway was quite dark. Behind Bertie was the smashed glass and frame where the Lithuanians escaped. Light came in. On the left side they got the rooms where they kept the wallpapers and tapestries and that. Upstairs they got furniture and books. Bertie was only worried about his stained glass.

'Bertie?' I went.

'Who is it?'

'You can come out now.'

Bridget got a snap of him coming out from under.

'They all gone?' he went trembling.

'They all gone now. This is the quiet time. Make the best of it. Soon you got an army coming in.'

'Army? Not more shooting?'

'Nah. Army of forensics. Photographers. Fingerprints. The lot Bertie.'

'I don't know what's happening. I don't know anything these days. Was it them bloody kids again?'

'It was Old Bill Bertie. And New Bill. And a few gangsters.'

'They stole my postcards!'

On the way out by his desk the Lithuanians lifted a few cards from the stand. Souvenirs maybe. Where they spent their holidays.

'Disgusting Bertie. Bleeding disgusting. Never be allowed.'

'Is the stained glass intact?'

'Hope so mate. We go and take a butcher's.'

Then they came in numbers. Funny enough, it seemed they never wanted me and Bridget wandering about that museum now. Nor the trippers they still got in there clocked the whole proceedings, couple of Dutch, couple of Japanese and a few schoolkids. They told us all fuck off out.

They found one Lithuanian upstairs while we were there. Took him out on a stretcher. He seemed like a bit alive, a bit dead.

So two got away.

We counted four Old Bill went down on the street.

Oh and Jimmy Foley got winged again. Why he lagged behind. Piece of shrapnel, only a ricochet, broke his arm.

Rameez and his boys long since made a disappearance. We walked past their barriers by the Bell. Motors burning now.

Then Bridget went running for her office fast as her little pins could carry her. I went home.

THIRTY-ONE

WE SAT THERE next day in my gaff.

Noreen took time off, flex time. She was pouring rum and tea.

Rameez on his tod.

Bridget Tansley.

George my warrant.

Jimmy Foley, arm in a sling.

And DS TT Holdsworth.

'Nicky the time is right for a de-briefing,' he reckoned when he belled me.

'Fair enough TT,' I went. 'Like you tell me what the fuck going down or what?'

'Perhaps. If we know. It is felt from above that you are due an explanation.'

So he came round and I got Bridget for a witness, case he brought the squad and they took me down Chingford for a kicking. But it was only him and his briefcase.

And he was looking kind of sad, staring in his cup of tea like there was someone he wanted to arrest in there.

George though he was like a bear in the woods. Ever since he got squeezed out of the Old Bill George was never a happy geezer. Till now when they started shooting each other. He opened up with the tactful questioning.

'So you really fucked up, TT, am I right?' he went.

'We have pointed up some failures of procedure,' TT goes. 'With the benefit of hindsight we appreciate that we might have pursued different lines of enquiry.'

'Like who was the bent copper? Who was doing the deals?'

'Fortunately the outcome was ultimately satisfactory. We have arrested the perpetrators. All of them. We think.'

'And what about you?' George went. 'How do you come out of this?'

'Ah well. Well. Fortunately an isolated error of judgement, a failing in lateral vision, is viewed in today's Police Service as a learning opportunity and is not allowed to mask the wider scenario of a promising career.'

In other words TT came up smelling of roses.

'So who was involved, TT?' went Bridget. She was like

a rabbit after the fish. 'Was Finlay on the take?'

'Well, yes, we have to acknowledge that Finlay was, as you put it, on the take. I suppose he was, let me put it like this, he was sharing the proceeds of crime with the Lithuanians.'

He sipped his rosie. He was hoping we were happy now, get down the boozer for a pint and a packet of cheese and onion. Only we sat there waiting.

He cleared his throat.

'Carry on, TT,' went Bridget. Wanting her story.

'You want more?'

'I think you've hardly started. What about all the others? Where did they fit in? How much was he making?'

TT was shifting. He was never liking this.

We all clocked him. We were waiting.

He surrendered.

'It was large.'

'How much?'

'We don't know. In exchange for a percentage he was, as you can guess, not arresting the Lithuanians for their offences. But then he found himself under pressure from both sides. The squad wanted some arrests. They had a grass—'

'Jonas,' I goes.

'Jonas. And they had information but nothing seemed to be happening. It wasn't happening because Finlay was holding it off. It was building up.'

TT sipped his tea. He was cream crackered. He was used to pulling in the news not giving it out.

'Then Jonas got shafted,' I went.

'Then Jonas was murdered. But when the murder was committed it all blew up and the guvnor had to have action. If your grass gets murdered you will never get another grass. The situation was out of control. They went too far. Something had to be done. That was when he thought of you, Nicky.'

'Like he made me an offer.'

'Yes.'

'Grass someone up so it never came from him.'

'Exactly.'

'And they come after me instead.'

'Nicky the Police Service feels that an acknowledgment will be due and must be forthcoming.'

'And my poor mate Jimmy here.'

'Yeah!' goes Jimmy, right as rain now except where he was leaking from his exit wounds.

'Compensation,' I goes. Everyone sat up. I was none too sure what I wanted compensation for except it sounded like the right word. Rameez was fidgeting. Felt a percentage coming on. 'And for Jimmy,' I goes, feeling a percentage myself.

'But then,' carries on TT rolling like a runaway now, 'DI Finlay was assaulted.'

'Smacked.'

'The Lithuanians were paying him to make sure there were no arrests. They suspected he was wavering. This was their reminder to him. Or to others.'

'But it backfired on them,' went Bridget.

'They hit him too hard. They put him in hospital and DI McAllen came in from the Yard to take his place. And he was not happy about anything, including, Nicky, the money given to you.

'He never reckoned what was happening?'

'Not at first. There were others involved, we think, and they obscured the situation. Then you left for Lithuania.'

'Short holiday. Winter break.'

'And you saw Jonas's widow.'

Silence in the gaff.

'Then you came back again. By which time the pressure was so great that arrests had to be made. Anyone. And something had to be done about you.'

'Finlay got me seen in Lithuania.'

'Finlay came out of hospital quite quickly. He heard you had left Walthamstow. It was easy to find out that you'd gone to Lithuania. He contacted the police there. And he contacted the villains.'

'So I got to be whacked.'

'Yes.'

Bit of a toecurler. Someone never liked me. We all sipped our drinks.

'And they still never got anyone for Jonas,' went Bridget.

'Not yet. But I think they will do.'

'So then,' Bridget went on, 'Finlay tried to sort everyone out at Walthamstow police station. A desperate last resort.' She was getting excited was Bridget. She got it all worked out. 'Bring it all to a head. Get the firearms people in. Nicky identifies the Lithuanians, the Lithuanians murder Nicky having failed in Lithuania, the police try to arrest the Lithuanians, the Lithuanians shoot at them so the police gun them down. Finlay gets rid of both Nicky and the Lithuanians. And no-one remembers what led up to it all. Nobody who was a witness is left alive anyway.'

'I'm afraid so.'

We all got to have a good drink on that one.

'Only,' I goes, 'my mate George here came good on the precautionals.'

'Fortunately,' George goes, 'I still happen to play golf with a couple of high-ups at the Met sports club. I was able to go to the top.'

'They best give you a start for that golf next time George. Owe you a few holes on that course I reckon.'

'I can beat them anyway,' he went smirking.

Then TT reached in his briefcase.

'There will be no compensation from the police,' he went firm.

I forgot about that compensation.

'There will be no admission of liability.'

Jimmy was starting to shiver. He was never fitted with a

five-speed brainbox was Jimmy, only when he smelled money he got the basic instincts of a rat.

'But I have here two application forms for compensation for the victims of crime.'

I started to giggle. Couldn't help myself. I loved a bribe.

'And we in the Police Service will undertake to fast track this application to the very best of our ability.'

By now the whole lot of us were cackling out loud. I was afraid Rameez might injure himself on his blade. I poured out more rum. I even got the chocolate biscuits out.

Then the dog rang.

Noreen took it.

Got a glint in her mincers straight off. Passed me the piece.

'Yeah?' I went.

'Nicky this is Helga.'

'YES!' I went sudden and loud. 'YES YES YES YES!'

'Ah!' She cackled she was so pleased. 'You are happy to hear from me, yes?'

'Yeah!' About to turn round and say her name, bit it off.

'I will not talk for so long.'

'Bound to be listening.'

'I understand. You will ring me from another number?'

'Correct.'

'I am thinking that I would like to take a short holiday in England. Is it possible that I may come to see you?'

'Yes!'

'Very good. I shall expect your call.'

'It come soon.'

We both rang off. I kept it all to myself. I reckoned I might get a seizure though.

I poured another rum.

'You will not forget my assist of course Nicky,' goes Rameez. Like Jimmy he could smell good news.

'Course not Rameez. Course not mate.'

'What I was thinking.'

'Noreen,' I goes gentle, kind of gracious.

'Yes Nicky?'

'You fancy a good night out? Couple of drinks, game of pool, get a takeaway? All on me?'

'You know how to treat a girl Nicky.'

'Once in a while Noreen, splash out, touch you like a princess.'

'You afford it Nicky?'

'I reckon so,' I went.

I poured more rum for everyone.